RENEGADE LEGIONNAIRE

General Sturmer, formerly a Nazi officer in the German desert forces, now leads a group of renegade Arab headhunters, tracking down Foreign Legion deserters — a lucrative business. Meanwhile, ex-cowboy Legionnaire Texas is planning revenge. He aims to capture Sturmer and bring him to face justice in America for his war crimes. In Tunisia, during the war, Sturmer had been responsible for the deaths of thousands of prisoners . . . and one of them had been Tex's brother . . .

GORDON LANDSBOROUGH

RENEGADE LEGIONNAIRE

Complete and Unabridged

LINFORD
Leicester

First published in Great Britain

First Linford Edition
published 2012

British Library CIP Data

Landsborough, Gordon.
 Renegade legionnaire. - -
 (Linford mystery library)
 1. Suspense fiction.
 2. Large type books.
 I. Title II. Series
 823.9'14–dc23

 ISBN 978–1–4448–1149–0

Published by
F. A. Thorpe (Publishing)
Anstey, Leicestershire

Set by Words & Graphics Ltd.
Anstey, Leicestershire
Printed and bound in Great Britain by
T. J. International Ltd., Padstow, Cornwall

This book is printed on acid-free paper

1

About noon the cavalcade of Arab horsemen joined the main Arab army massing north of the burnt-out fortress at El Kwatra.

There was a tremendous excitement when it became known that the Arab nationalist leader, Abdul el Nuhas, was in the party having returned from exile in Egypt to lead the resentful tribesmen against the French who ruled over their land.

They came surging round, brown faces alight with enthusiasm, fighting to touch the hem of his gold-embroidered cloak. He was a fine figure of a man, that Arab warrior chief, broad and strong, bold-looking and resolute. He was just the man the Arabs needed for the fight to throw the despotic infidel back across the sea from whence he had come

A tent had been set up, ready to receive their leader, and the escort of horsemen fought a clear passage through the milling, burnoused Arabs, so that Nuhas Pasha could ride across to it. The chieftain dismounted, his magnificent horse was led away by an attendant, and he went inside to receive the homage of the local sheiks.

With his departure, the attention of the crowd was diverted to the rest of his party. They saw, amongst that dismounting, fierce-eyed bodyguard that had ridden escort over their leader for at least six hundred miles across the desert wastes, one man who was not an Arab.

He was a big, lean, hardy-looking man who sat his horse as easily as any of these Arab warriors. And he sat at ease, too, as if unconcerned about his safety, though he wore the uniform of the people who were enemies of the Arabs

He was a Legionnaire. His tunic was soiled and torn, yet it was the blue tunic of the French Foreign Legion; his trousers were even more desert-stained, yet they were the white issue drill that was the marching uniform of the Legion.

The Arabs, thronging around that gaily

decorated tent in which their chiefs conferred, looked at the Legionnaire and their eyes grew fierce. Here would be a prisoner picked up by Nuhas Pasha on his journey across the desert. He would die, of course, they thought, as all dogs of infidels should die.

And then they noticed something — that the Legionnaire was no prisoner, as they had thought. For prisoners did not usually carry Lebel rifles across their saddle bows, nor have six-shot revolvers holstered about their waists.

It puzzled them, and sharp, guttural Arab voices shouted questions at the escort. The replies silenced them. This Legionnaire was no prisoner. He had come voluntarily with the party, and Nuhas Pasha had said that no man's hand should be raised against him.

A renegade, was the thought in the Arab's minds at that. A traitor, like many others, they decided contemptuously, and they turned their backs upon the man who was safe from their swords and returned to the business of talking about the next phase of this desert rebellion.

The tall Legionnaire seemed unmindful of the Arabs and their expressions of contempt. He looked to his horse and then attended to his own comfort. With the other Arabs, the picked bodyguard that had ridden in with Nuhas Pasha, he seemed on good terms, and they all sat in a group and shared hard, brown bread, and ate dried figs and dates and some cucumbers that were brought to them by the local tribesmen.

They called him 'Texas', and when he spoke there was a nasal quality to his uncertain Arabic that told of the American.

After a time word came out that Nuhas Pasha and his chiefs wanted to speak with the Legionnaire. Tex rose slowly from the hot, desert sand, knocked his pants free from the clinging grains, and then tramped slowly in his heavy Legion boots over to the tent.

It had been opened, after the first greeting with the chiefs, so that all who wished could listen to the conference of their leaders, for that is the Arab way.

Now Tex saw a wide-open tent that

4

provided shade only for the principals. Vivid-coloured carpets were outspread, and upon them squatted the burnoused Arab chiefs, with their gold-ringed *agals* denoting their rank, and rich silk ceremonial robes making a bold display of colour against the background of black, goat-skinned tent. The standard of the Arab army was flying, making the scene gay under that blue semi-tropical sky.

Before the chiefs squatted a hundred Arabs in the sand, spectators ready to join in the debate if they felt like it. Tex saw everywhere brown eyes watching him, saw bearded, brown faces turned towards his as he stepped over their legs and faced the leaders on those bright carpets.

Nuhas Pasha greeted him with friendliness. He had the rich brown, pointed beard of a man in his prime, and was handsome — and knew it. This was the first time that ex-Legionnaire Tex had had a chance to speak with him, for he had only joined the party the previous evening.

At the greeting, the big American

squatted down Arab-fashion with his hosts. All the chiefs were looking curiously at him, for it was unusual to have an enemy in their midst.

Nuhas Pasha said, courteously, 'It is the will of our people that you should help them against the enemy they hate.' Tex was silent. Nuhas went on, 'Three nights ago they attacked the French Foreign Legion Post at El Kwatra. All were killed who were within, and the post was burned to the ground, as we saw this day.'

Tex continued to listen politely. Substantially the chief was correct, of course, but not entirely. Tex knew better than he, for he had been within the fortress when it was attacked — had been, in fact, in a prison cell at the moment when treachery permitted the Arabs entry into the fortress.

He had been lucky to escape over the wall in the fighting — had been luckier still, almost at once, to throw an Arab off his horse and flee towards the south on that sturdy mount

Yes, not all had been killed of the garrison.

For instance, Ca-ca hadn't been killed; neither had Mervin Petrie, the executioner's assistant from Marseilles, nor Dwarf Quelclos who was only half a man but twice as savage. And Cheauvin the Weeper, a Belgian, had got away, and the Bulgar with his bad teeth and fouler temper.

And worst of them all, La Femme, who looked maidenly and innocent but was viciousness incarnate within.

They'd been in that garrison, that fateful night, but they'd escaped with their lives. For it was they who had handed over the fortress to the Legion's enemies. In the night, when they should have been on guard, by prearranged plan they had lifted the big main gate and permitted the wild Arab tribesmen to flood in. The garrison, trusting to their comrades on the ramparts, had been killed, many before they were quite out of their beds in the whitewashed barrack rooms.

Now, Tex was thinking, the renegades and traitors would be enjoying the rewards of their treachery. They'd be on their way to some port that would give passage across to the Europe they missed and craved for. They'd be under safe escort of Arab horsemen, their pockets, no doubt, filled with gold that would be part of the reward for their services.

Yeah, he thought cynically, crime sometimes did pay, though that was the biggest and blackest crime he had ever heard of.

The sun burned on that lean, brown Texan's face as he sat and let his thoughts flash back to the momentous night of a few days before. He let the sand trickle through his fingers, as Nuhas Pasha went on calmly, confidently detailing his requirements. Nuhas Pasha, exiled rebel leader now returned to his own country, was very sure that what he wanted would be.

'Before that accursed French fortress was destroyed all arms and ammunition, as well as equipment, was obtained by our gallant warriors. Among these arms were four machine guns. You, O Legionnaire, will instruct my men in the use of those so deadly weapons.'

Tex lifted his head at that. His thought had drifted away to the oasis called Bir Khula, sixty miles south of them. For they were his comrades — Dimmy Dimicci, who had been wounded and was the reason why they were resting in that oasis; Rube Koskowsci — The Schemer — bright-eyed and always full of plans; and flat-faced, good tempered Joe Ellighan, his closest buddy of the Legion.

And with them was a girl . . .

Clearly, unhesitatingly. Tex said, 'I shall teach no one how to use any machine guns.'

Nuhas Pasha's handsome, brown-bearded face didn't lose its smile but his voice became just a little too hearty.

'Last night you asked permission to ride north with my party. I promised you safe conduct because you had saved the life of one of our people.' That dignified head inclined slightly. 'That will be done, in spite of what you say now. But there is much that intrigues me, O Westerner. It is in my mind to know what mission you are undertaking.'

So Tex told him — told all those listening Arabs.

'I joined the Foreign Legion not to find a place of refuge, not to escape from justice or a bad wife, as so many of my comrades did. Neither was I interested in war; I had had enough of that in the fighting in North Africa against the German and Italian armies.

'I thought the desert was quiet, that I would be on garrison duty and there would be no wars and fighting.' He gestured towards the lines of tents that marked the camping ground of this swelling army of Arabs. 'I was not to know that Arab nationalism would so soon take up arms again.'

A bearded, old warrior in the assembly growled, 'Always we shall take to the sword whilst the accursed Frank rules our country. Never will there be lasting peace!'

A savage, thick-throated murmur rose from the others. Plainly that was a popular sentiment.

Tex waited until the noise subsided, and then he went on with his story.

'I joined the Legion for a purpose. That was to find a man who had done things that no man should. He killed my brother and a thousand other men of my country.' Tex found his hands gripping, though it was many years since that terrible crime.

'He was a general in the German army that operated here in North Africa. When the Allied armies began to drive them out of Tunisia, that German general did something that has since shocked the world. He killed his prisoners rather than that they should be released to fight against his harassed men. He killed them foully.'

But he didn't explain the crime of General Herman Sturmer — how the men had been held in a pit in the desert, and motor trucks had been backed to the edge and exhaust gases directed down through rubber pipes to poison the sleeping prisoners. He didn't tell how some — including his brother, on Sturmer's own admission — had wakened and tried to get out of the pit and had been mown down by machine gunners.

Tex went on, his voice quite steady again, 'That man I want to take to my own country, to be tried by the Allied War Crimes Commission. For years he was thought to be dead, and then it began to be whispered that there was an officer named Sturmer, a German, in the service of the French Foreign Legion. The Legion denied that it was the same Sturmer, but then they always do.'

Once a man joined the Legion, his past was forgotten. If the French listened to demands from other countries and permitted extradition, they would have an army considerably smaller than they had at present.

Sturmer was in the Legion, and apparently there was no power to get him out.

'I joined the Legion in the hope of meeting this man and identifying him. I planned to capture him and smuggle him out of this country.' Nuhas Pasha's dark eyebrows lifted at that bold talk. 'I did meet him. He is a leader of *partizans* — '

There was a stir and a gasp at that. The *partizans* were mostly renegade Arabs in the employ of France. They were the most vicious, degenerate of men, held in horror by Arab and Legionnaire alike.

For their job was to cut off heads and because they received bounties for the heads they brought in, they were not always careful in selecting them.

France employed them to roam the deserts, like fierce watchdogs, on the lookout for deserters from the Legion. They never brought in prisoners; always it was the head and *matricule* on which was the identity number. That was all.

And sometimes, it was said, they cut off Arab's heads, where they had found stolen identity numbers, and tried to get bounty on them, too.

'I tried to take him, along with my comrades, out of the desert but he escaped, thanks to the treachery of one of my friends.' He shrugged. 'Now, well I guess Sturmer's somewhere around,' he ended, lapsing into his native American at that.

Nuhas Pasha was watching the big, lean Texan curiously and intently all the while he was speaking. He was thinking that this man was a cut above the ordinary Legionnaire, who was mostly scum, anyway, for all his fighting proclivities.

For one thing, few Legionnaires could speak much Arabic, yet this one did fluently. True the Legionnaire had spoken of previous service in North Africa, during which time he might have made a study of the native language.

He was still, clearly, an intelligent man. He also thought, looking at that strong-moulded face, 'This man would make a bad enemy . . . '

Aloud, Nuhas Pasha said, 'May Allah be with you. A man should avenge the death of his brother.' A murmur of approval rose again from the crowd at that. An eye for an eye, and a tooth for a tooth. That was the way these desert wanderers looked upon life.

The Arab leader kept his bright, brown eyes on the Legionnaire. Tex, wise in the way of men, knew that this man wanted to persuade him into some course of action other than the one he, Tex, wished to pursue, yet was uncertain of how to broach the matter.

So Tex spoke again, decisively, to make matters even more clear.

'Though I have deserted from the Legion, I will not fight against my former comrades. I will not help you, either, with information or instruction in the use of the arms you have captured.'

There was an Arab sheik there who was restless, who kept turning the while Tex was speaking. He had a mean, brooding way of looking at the ex-Legionnaire that Tex hadn't missed.

Now he spoke, and his voice trembled with belly anger. 'This is a bold dog, to speak thus. Does he not know that we are the enemies of all who wear that accursed uniform? Does he not know that we kill when we see that blue tunic?'

Tex heard that guttural, savage Arab voice. He got the drift of what the sheik said, and he promptly replied, 'Does this warrior chief not know that the word of an Arab is good? That if an Arab says, 'You are my friend; no harm will come to you' — no harm will come upon you? I have placed myself in the hands of Nuhas

15

Pasha, and I am content.'

Nuhas spoke calmly, 'Your life is in my hands. I hold all men responsible to me.' But even so, he was not beyond trying again. 'Yet if you should think differently; if you would become a true friend and join our cause, there would be honour and wealth for you. You would become a man among men and a chieftain in your own right.'

Tex merely answered, 'I want one thing — Sturmer. I want to get to that fiend and put him on the stand to face justice. There's nothing else I want.'

Certainly not wealth. He had a ranch back in Texas that could provide him with all the comforts he so little needed. Not rank. He didn't want to become a damn' sheik!

And he also thought, 'It wouldn't last, anyway. The French are too strong . . . '

This undisciplined, poorly equipped Arab army, for all its fanatical fighting qualities, couldn't stand against the superior forces of the French. For a time they might have victories, but in the end there could be only defeat for the Arabs.

He rose, having made his decision and expressed it in careful Arabic, and went back to his place with the bodyguard. As he walked among the seated warriors, there were many who drew back, as if the blue uniform he wore held the quality of disease about it.

Without apparently looking, he yet saw the eyes that lifted from some of them — hating eyes. In spite of what Nuhas Pasha had said, that he held all men responsible to him for the safety of the Legionnaire's life, he knew that among that audience and in that army were many who would end his life at the first opportunity.

Too many had cause to identify that blue uniform with appalling suffering . . .

★　★　★

Half an hour before sundown, when it was already becoming cool, Tex said goodbye to his companions of the trail that day, Nuhas Pasha's bodyguard, and headed northwards through the sprawling Arab camp and thence beyond into the clean yellow desert.

There was some friendliness from the bodyguard, but none from the Arab warriors who squatted in groups outside their ungainly tents of black goatskin. Most looked with apathy at him, but there were a few who grew fierce-eyed and growled that this was a dog of a Legionnaire who would be fighting against them perhaps within a matter of hours.

They argued, that in spite of Nuhas Pasha's pledge, perhaps it would be better if someone cut that accursed throat for the infidel, like the unclean pig he was.

But they argued only, those men at the tents. Nuhas Pasha was not a man to cross lightly.

There were three who did take the trail after the American Legionnaire, however. They were the followers of the sheik with the mean, brooding look and fierce, resentful eyes. A thin man in a race of thin men, with the thinness that comes to men who are ever busy with momentous schemes.

He was a man jealous of Nuhas Pasha,

anyway, because the returned warrior from Egypt had deposed him as head of the Arab army.

He clapped his hands and a lieutenant came leaping up at the summons. 'Go thou,' said Sheik Mahmoud ibn Kalim ibn Hussein ibn Achmen el Dusa. 'Take two men and put an end to that dog of a Legionnairre.'

The startled lieutenant whispered. 'It was Nuhas Pasha's orders . . . ' His eyes drifted uneasily past his thin, evil-eyed master to the sheiks' tent, wherein still sat the war leader of the Arab nationalists.

Sheik Mahmoud snapped, 'I say go! Art thou my servant, or dost thou earn thy salt with another?' His fingers impetuously clenched about the ornamented silver handgrip of his *flissa*, that dreaded sword of the desert nomad.

His lieutenant salaamed deeply, and began to retreat. Sheik Mahmoud flung further angry words after him. He was a man who grew fierce at the slightest frustration to his plans; and this night he was even more than usually touchy.

No general likes demotion. No man

who has tasted power likes to hand over to another. He went back to his tent, and there sat and plotted against Nuhas Pasha.

His lieutenant called two men. He called angrily, because it is the way of lieutenants to pass on the stings and blows of their superiors. His men grumbled in their beards and, because there was nothing else for them to take it out of, they were vicious in the use of their spurs upon their horses.

For Sheik Mahmoud had said, 'Your life is forfeit if you fail to kill that infidel.'

Tex rode eastward. When he was out of sight of that vast army encamped on the broad, flat desert, he spurred hard and rode as fast as the rock soil would permit. And when it began to grow dark, he turned his horse's head northwards.

For Tex was experienced in desert strategy. He had guessed that someone among those thousands might seek to disobey his master and come after him to slay him because he had not been an Arab. He struck north and still rode hard for an hour in the darkness, at the end of which time he knew no pursuit would follow.

He rested for a few hours, because he had ridden in the heat of the sun all day, but by four in the morning, long before the eastern horizon began to silhouette before the rising sun, he was on his way again.

He had crossed the Arab lines. Now he was in No-man's Land. He expected to run into French forces within the next day or two.

Tex had planned to desert the Legion, hoping to be able to capture his enemy, ex-Nazi General Sturmer, on the way out; but with Sturmer's escape he had changed his plans. Now he was heading back towards the Legion.

No one would know he had tried to desert — only Sturmer himself knew that, and Sturmer wouldn't detect him once he was back within the Legion again ... wouldn't suspect his return and so wouldn't be looking for him among the thousands of men.

That would give Tex a chance to plan afresh to take the *partizan* captive and ride him south to join his waiting comrades at the oasis Bir Khula.

Tex thought of those good comrades of his as he rode northwards through the paling dawn. But especially he thought of the girl who was with them.

Her name was Nicky Shaw — Monica Shaw — and she was a New York newspaper woman. Her editor had sent her to try to get a scoop. 'Check on Sturmer rumour,' he had cabled. 'Get pictures.'

All America wanted to catch up with Sturmer for his brutality towards their kinsfolk. If Nicky Shaw could smuggle pictures out of the country, proving the real identity of the French Foreign Legion captain, Herman Sturmer, it would be the scoop of the century.

Well, the girl had secured such pictures, and now she was lying at the oasis Bir Khula, befriended by the Arab sheik who ruled that territory, and whose son's life Tex had saved. When Dimmy Dimicci, who had been badly wounded, recovered, the sheik had promised to escort them to the coast.

Tex sighed, remembering Nicky Shaw. She was lovely. Anyone could have these dark, exotic, North African beauties, but for him he'd take the cool loveliness of blonde, blue-eyed Nicky Shaw! She had humour and was a good sport, and on the journey across the desert she hadn't shown fear — only when the *partizans*, those ferocious Arab headhunters, were almost on top of them.

Tex had been mighty scared then, himself, he admitted wryly . . .

All day he let his horse plod across that burning desert waste. There were no landmarks in that vast, rolling land of dry, yellow sand. Just mound after mound, hill after hill of shifting soil that made progress as slow as it was hard.

Tex rode by his shadow. In the middle morning it was on his left. Towards noon he let it creep out in front of him; and in the afternoon it began to move down towards his right, as the sun descended in the far west. That way he knew he was heading roughly north. That way, eventually, he knew he must come to the coast and the garrison towns of the French

Foreign Legion, if he did not encounter outposts beforehand.

All he hoped was that his water wouldn't run out. He was drinking sparingly, and giving his horse none at all. A mouthful was nothing to the beast, but it could keep life in his own body for a few hours more.

Towards evening he topped a hill and found himself looking down upon an Arab village. There was water in the place, he knew, otherwise there wouldn't have been this cluster of mud hovels stuck in the middle of the desert.

He saw a few ragged palm trees, that seemed to wilt in the heat of the sun; saw dark green vegetation and cultivated strips of soil where irrigation channels must have been dug.

His horse grew excited as it smelled the water, and began to trot forward without any encouragement from his master. Tex let the stallion go where it wanted. He was watching that village and saw no signs of life. All the same he unslung his rifle, examined the barrel to see that no sand clogged it, and went down towards the village with his finger on the trigger.

There wasn't an Arab to be seen in the fields or throughout the buildings of the village. Tex thought, 'The men have all gone to join Nuhas Pasha's army.' In this godforsaken land, war was a wonderful excuse to leave the monotony of an existence, which hadn't changed for the desert inhabitants in ten thousand years.

Fighting the infidel, in any event, had been a national sport for many hundreds of years. What Arab with blood in his veins was going to miss it?

The cattle had gone. There were no goats, no camels, no sheep — above all, no mangy scavenger dogs to greet him as he approached the village. That told him there were none of the original inhabitants left. The womenfolk must have driven their flocks away out of this fighting zone.

Tex didn't know it, but he had stumbled upon the only waterhole within hundreds of square miles. The inhabitants had been well aware of this, knew it would be a military objective, and got out.

Tex merely thought, 'The hell, I sure am in luck, findin' water an' no one about to say I can't have none.'

What he wasn't to know was that that waterhole was like a crossroads in the desert. Whichever way traffic went, it headed through the waterhole so as to pick up life-giving supplies for the rest of the journey.

Someone was already in occupation.

As he came cautiously into the centre of the village where the headman had lived in a flat-roofed house that stood isolated in the wide-open space that was like a village square, there came a stir from watching men, who had seen him on the hilltop.

Then a man moved to a doorway and stood exposed to the view of the horseman. Another came quietly to the doorway opposite. As the horseman reined back his mount, four more silent, triumphant men came out behind ex-Legionnaire Tex.

Five and a half men — because one was only half a man.

They wore Arab burnouses, but these were parted in front, revealing the blue tunic of the Legionnaire. And guns were in their hands — Lebel rifles — and they were pointed at the heart of the big American who had once been a cow-wrangler.

2

A harsh voice shouted, '*Halte!* Move, you vile *bleu*, and you will be shot from the saddle!'

Tex soothed his startled horse with one hand; the Lebel was gripped tightly in the other, but he knew it was useless to try to use it. He had seen those levelled rifles, had recognized those faces, and knew he would die before the gun came inches high.

His grey eyes were narrowed, not so much to keep out the westering sun but to hide his thoughts from his enemies.

For these were men who would gladly see him die.

They were the renegade deserters — the men who had betrayed Fort El Kwatra to the enemy in return for safe conduct across the desert to the seaports.

The leader was Ca-ca. Tex looked at him. Long-faced, sallow, always dirty-looking. With coarse, black hair that left grease marks in his cap, on his pillow, and anywhere he rested his head. He was an Apache, a vicious Paris cutthroat, holding sway over brutal men because he could be more brutal, more ready with his fists and feet . . . and knife. Tex looked at that long nose, at those brown, gleaming eyes that were alight with satisfaction and cruelty, and knew that it had been a mistake to seek water in this village. Much more comfortable to die of thirst in the desert . . .

Ca-ca said softly, evilly, 'Oh, thou pig of an American, this night will live in your memory — as your worst on earth!'

He leapt forward at that, unable to restrain the fury in his savage, vengeful soul. This Texan had thrashed him and humbled him before his followers and been the means of a day in the cells, back at El Kwatra fortress. Ca-ca of the mean and hating soul wasn't the man to forgive that.

Now he swung his gun, butt coming over his shoulder, his soul afire at the thought of the things he would do to this big, rangy American before he died.

Tex jerked back, but too late. The heavy butt smacked him on the side of the head — a glancing blow because of his quick movement, but one sufficient to send him toppling from his saddle. He fell into the dust, and lay for a second, stunned.

Ca-ca kicked him. Then he kicked him again. The other men came closing in. They wanted to kick ex-Legionnaire Tex, too.

La Femme was first to get his blow in after Ca-ca. La Femme would. He had the face of an angel, of a lovely girl, but his was the soul of the devil. He liked inflicting cruelty, yet the world wouldn't have guessed it from his big, innocent blue eyes, so like a maiden's, or from the smooth, rounded cheeks that had never known the touch of a coarsening razor. He kicked, but Tex had begun to roll and the blow was lost in the movement.

He was dazed, but recovering his wits. He was trying to think. There was something he should remember, something that might turn the tables on these men . . .

Dwarf Quelclos kicked out and screamed at the same time. He couldn't forgive the world for making him so small, and accordingly he was never at peace with himself or his companions.

The Bulgar, foul of breath and rotten in teeth, cursed and swung his gun at the Texan. Cheauvin the Belgian, whose eye wept continuously, struck out with his fist as Tex swayed to his feet in spite of the savage attack.

Tex was still trying to remember, was trying to get the mistiness from his eyes following that first, smarting blow. He began to see, began to remember . . .

Mervin Petrie, who had left France because he had made himself a suitable candidate for the guillotine block, came in with a run — Mervin Petrie who had been assistant to the executioner at Marseilles until that little indiscretion when he'd beaten to death a man old enough to be his father — and was.

Mervin Petrie stopped dead in his tracks. For Tex had remembered . . . remembered and for a second was able to turn the tables on these men who had been lurking in that otherwise deserted Arab village.

He was a Legionnaire, but he carried a revolver on his thigh — that was what he remembered. That was something those renegades hadn't expected. Legionnaires carried Lebel rifles but never revolvers. When that rifle had fallen from the Texan's hands, they had considered him unarmed and it was safe for them to go in and punch and kick him until they were satisfied.

Now they stopped, rocking on their heels, as a revolver appeared in the Texan's hands . . .

That was something they never understood. One second and there was nothing in the Texan's hands. The next, a revolver, big, blue-barrelled and sinister, was there — and they never saw the movement in between that brought the gun from holster to hand.

It was the first time in their lives that they had witnessed the celebrated Texas lightning draw, and Tex was as good an exponent as any to demonstrate it.

Ca-ca shouted, '*Ohé!*' and sprang back

in alarm. That jostled his companions. They had guns in their hands, but all were pointing away from the hard-faced, crouching American, and none dared try to swing them round because that blue-barrelled gun said they would die even as the movement began.

Tex shouted, 'Get back, you swine!' He wanted to throw away this gun, wanted to go walking in with his fists flying, and thrash them one by one. But he didn't throw away his gun because that would have been rank folly.

For they wouldn't have thrown away theirs.

He shouted, 'Drop them guns, blast you!' But none obeyed. There wasn't one of them dared level his gun, but they were bold and knew he couldn't make them drop their weapons. If he opened fire, that would start them firing, too.

It was a bold bluff, but they dared him. They stood in that dusty open space among the stinking Arab hovels, tensed and crouched, eyes fixed on that lone figure that had so unexpectedly surprised them.

Tex licked his lips. His horse had cantered away and wasn't even in sight. He knew he couldn't open fire and kill all these men before some of them got their guns blasting and killed him. And they wouldn't put down their guns . . . They were just waiting for that fatal moment when his attention became diverted.

Tex started to go backwards, to where his Lebel was. He would need that, soon. He picked it up, eyes never leaving those six, silent figures, just waiting to shoot the life out of him.

Then he went backwards farther still, moving to an opening among the flat-roofed mud houses. He gained the corner in safety. Hesitated. Then ran for his life behind the houses.

A shot screamed over his shoulder as he tore towards the end of a cluster of huts that had been built together for support. He started to dive; to get into cover quickly before the next shots came. Four spanged almost simultaneously above him, but he had saved himself with that fall.

It took the skin off his elbows, but he

never felt it, never knew it till later. He just lurched to his feet and ran on, zig-zagging when he crossed open ground, but mostly ducking from cover to cover through the village. As he ran he cursed. That damn' horse . . . where'n Hades had it run to?

All at once he was through the last of the buildings. He found himself under palm trees that scraped dry leaves together with an unmusical sound — like the rubbing of palsied old hands, he found himself thinking.

A system of irrigation ditches, bisecting small, intensively cultivated vegetable plots, stretched before him. He saw cucumbers, tomatoes, melons, egg fruit, peppers . . . rich vegetation that was dying because no one was there to keep the irrigation channels clear and permit the life-giving water to flow through.

He saw a streambed to his right that was deeper than these irrigation channels and promised better cover. He swerved and crashed into the water just before Ca-ca and Mervin Petrie ran into view, their Arab cloaks streaming behind them.

Ca-ca hadn't seen where Tex had gone, but he must have guessed.

Tex heard the harsh voice, filled with the accents of the Paris gutters. Ca-ca shouted, 'Search the houses, *mes amis*. Mervin and I will search these fields!'

Ca-ca wanted to kill Tex. Knew he had to kill him. Though the ex-cowpuncher at the time didn't understand why. Just at that moment Tex was thinking, 'Sure, he wants to kill me. Ca-ca's a killer, all right. Cross Ca-ca an' your throat's as good as cut — if you'll let him.'

But there was more to it than that.

Ca-ca and his renegades were in a desperate plight. They had been promised escort to the coast following their betrayal of the fortress and their comrades, and the Arabs had tried to keep their word. The only thing was, warning had got through to the coast before them, telling of the destruction of the desert outpost.

One of the Legionnaires who had escaped the slaughter had somehow managed to secure a horse and had raced through the Arab forces and reached Sidi-bel Illah, the big Legion garrison town.

At once the French troops were mobilised. Ca-ca and his Arab escort had found marching columns of men everywhere ahead of them, all moving southwards and barring the way to the coast.

They had, in fact, run into a patrol of Colonial native troops and been fired at, and that had turned them and sent them back to this waterhole in the desert. There the Arab escort had left them. After all, this was as far as they could take them; that unexpected warning of the coast troops had completely stopped all plans of escape.

Ca-ca and his renegades had been discussing their situation when they had sighted the lone Legionnaire on the distant hill. They were desperate men. They had sought to escape the Legion because life had been hell for them and they had craved for the fleshpots of the capitals of Europe. But even life in the Legion was preferable to death against a wall before a firing party.

Now, racing after Tex through that Arab village a sudden, startling thought had come to Ca-ca.

If Tex died, no one would know they had played the renegade. He was the only witness, the only man who had been awake, and watching when they lifted the big fortress gate to the Arab invaders.

'Legionnaire Tek-suss must die,' Ca-ca had promptly shouted to his comrades. Then, if they couldn't find a way of escape from the Legion, they could ride up boldly and claim to be survivors from the fort at El Kwatra.

'Tek-suss must die,' the American heard him shout harshly. He began to move cautiously between the banks of this stream that began as a bubbling spring and ended its life after less than half a mile in the shifting sands of the desert.

He was stooping, though the water was nearly up to his waist. When he bent nearly double he was below the level of the grass-lined banks, though he caught occasional glimpses of Mervin and Ca-ca through the vegetation.

His idea became — get as far away from the village as possible. When that was done, perhaps he could surprise the two renegades and put them out of action before the other four came up to help. If he were lucky he might dispose of the gang, and then the fight would become more on equal terms.

Separate and then destroy! That had been one of the axioms of desert warfare, he remembered

So he plunged up that winding streambed, while behind him floundered the other renegade Legionnaires. It was hard going, and treacherous, because the bottom of the stream was uneven and covered with a smooth silt that tried to hold his feet wherever he put them.

Then came disaster, at a moment when three men, riding towards the tiny oasis, dismounted from their horses at sight of the two running Legionnaires in the vegetable fields.

They were Arabs, the followers of the Sheik Mahmoud, who wanted to be a leader of men and hated to have to follow another.

Tex ran into a pocket in the streambed. It was a couple of feet deeper than the rest of the stream, but it was the unexpectedness of it that threw him off balance. He found himself going down, deeper than before; tried to pull himself back — and went totally under water.

That meant that neither his rifle nor his revolver was any good now.

He came up, spluttering and cursing, though silently. His Lebel, still firmly gripped in his left hand, was a thing of mud and running water. The revolver on his hip was also caked in oozy slime.

Ca-ca heard him, heard something, anyway. He came running straight towards that bend in the stream, Petrie following. Their Arab cloaks were flung wide, showing the uniforms underneath; their Lebels clutched at the ready, able to spray lead at a fraction of a second's warning.

Tex, peering through the water that ran down from his kepi, looking cautiously over the edge of the bank, saw the two Legionnaires, saw the look of murder on their faces, and knew he was in as tight a spot as he'd ever been.

At which precise moment, a shot rang out from behind him. Not a crisp explosion, such as came from a modern

Lebel, but a rounder, duller roar, as from some old muzzle-loader that hadn't been packed tight with the ramrod. A bullet lobbed over Tex's head, aimed for the oncoming pair, but missed by a mile.

Tex shook the mud out of his eyes and wheeled. He saw three Arabs standing back among the trees. He took a chance and shouted, 'Friend!' in Arabic. One of the Arabs beckoned quickly.

Ca-ca and Mervin Petrie had gone diving into cover with that first ineffective shot. The other two Arabs emptied their old guns and made them keep out of sight for a few seconds. Then the Bulgar appeared at a corner of one of the houses and began to empty his magazine at the Arabs across the fields. He was accurate with his fire and made the Arabs turn head over heels in a frantic effort to escape the spinning lead.

The other renegades came running out from the crazy, leaning, mud hovels that Tex would have called 'dobe', back in his own country. Probably Petrie and his leader, Ca-ca came up from cover then and started firing, for the air was filled

41

with a murderous hail of lead.

Tex clambered out of the stream, over a depression in the bank that was out of sight of the renegades. He found himself in a dried-up irrigation channel that led straight towards where he had last seen those Arabs, and he went along it like a crab, down as close to the mud as he could keep himself.

He still held his precious but useless Lebel, and it kept getting in the way, but he wouldn't drop it. Given time to get the dirt out of the barrel, it might yet save his life.

The sun poured on to him, though it was low down in the west and near to setting; he felt the hot rays burn on to the damp tunic, so that the water that trickled through to his skin felt warm. It was unpleasant, and he hoped his clothes would quickly dry.

At the end of the ditch, where tall sugar canes were planted to absorb the overflow of water, he stood up cautiously and peered around.

He saw blue uniforms dodging from cover to cover across the fields behind him. The renegades were coming up rapidly and overtaking him. They weren't more than eighty yards away, and that wasn't a safe lead.

Gasping for breath after his exertions, muddied to the peak of his kepi, he looked around desperately. He couldn't see the Arabs, whose timely arrival had, for the moment at least, saved his life.

He began to work his way through the sugar canes that were tall enough to give him cover. Abruptly he broke out from them and the ground grew harder and drier underfoot immediately. He had left the cultivated area and was in a wilderness of scrub thorns and menacing prickly-pear bushes and a few palm trees.

He ran on, dodging so as to keep under cover. Someone was crashing through the green sugar canes behind him, and he knew it would be one of the renegades, out to silence him.

The light grew brighter. He realized that he was on the edge of the oasis, and in a minute would be running on to the bare desert. He hesitated, not knowing which way to turn.

Then he saw the trio of Arabs again. They must have spotted him at the same time. They were about fifty yards out on to the desert, mounted and seeming about to put spurs to their mounts and flee.

When they saw the running Legionnaire, they halted. It seemed to Tex, coming to a suspicious stop suddenly, that they exchanged quick words. Then one shouted '*Taal!*' — come — and Tex jumped towards them.

He didn't know them, didn't understand why they should be friendly towards one who wore the hated blue of the Legion, but he felt he had little choice in the matter. If he stayed where he was, six murderous renegades, advancing rapidly upon him, would wipe him out in a matter of seconds.

He thought, 'Maybe these guys are from Nuhas Pasha's army. Maybe they saw me there and heard what Nuhas said — no one must harm me, because I saved an Arab's life.'

So he ran forward, slinging his rifle over his back as he did so. He raced from cover, up towards the three horsemen, just as they started to wheel away. He saw lean, brown faces, black-bearded and fierce-looking, peering down at him from under their white burnouses. He grabbed a stirrup and yelled, 'Get her goin', brother! Them varmints is within shootin' range!'

The Arabs seemed to understand, and went spurring away, Tex hanging on grimly and racing with giant strides alongside the racing mount . . .

The Arabs had recognized him, that was why they had offered to help him. For Sheik Mahmoud the Plotter had said, 'Your lives are forfeit if you fail to kill that cursed Legionnaire.'

Killing Tex would have been easy, several times in the last few minutes, especially just now when he had come racing out from the oasis towards them. But it would not have been sufficient for them to have killed the Legionnaire and then gone back and reported on their action to their chief. Sheiks were sometimes inclined to doubt a man's word, and before it could be confirmed that man's head might be off, or a bullet through his chest.

Those three wary Arabs had decided that proof must be taken back to their sheik that they had indeed achieved their objective. That proof . . . they would take the Legionnaire's head with them.

But to get a head, you must be within sword distance of your target, and until this moment, when Tex caught hold of the stirrup, there would have been no opportunity to secure their trophy.

Now . . . it was running obligingly alongside them.

3

A shot suddenly cracked out behind them. Lead stirred the air into a high-pitched scream. Running hard, Tex kept his head well down, because that bullet from the renegades hadn't been much higher than his kepi. A second later, a whole fusillade of shots came whistling after them, but only one shot hit and that merely stirred a horse into more frenzied speed, as the lead grazed a haunch.

They were pretty well at the extent of the Lebel's range, and running into safety with every stride. Another ten seconds and they would be well beyond range.

They made it, though a ragged volley followed them and kicked up dust clouds close on their heels. With that, simultaneously, the three Arab horsemen pulled their mounts down to a slow walk. They were safe.

Tex still held on, because he was

47

blown. He looked up, perspiration dripping from his hot, brown face. He caught the three Arabs looking at each other, but didn't understand the meaning of the glances. They were climbing a hill that was sand until near to the top, and then it became a solid block of sandstone rock that reared yellow-red and crumbling from out of the earth.

Tex called, 'I sure owe you some thanks, pards,' and then searched through his Arabic to make a reasonable translation.

One of the Arabs said, 'Allah was with you,' and then looked at his companions quickly, meaningfully. Tex realized that the men were stopping, almost where the sandstone reared like a wall out of the sand. More, suddenly, almost instinctively, he became aware that the horsemen were crowding in upon him, coming closer to him with their sweating, lather-stained steeds.

That was all at the moment — instinct — that warned him of danger, yet immediately he was alert, his eyes watching and his muscles tensed and ready.

He released that stirrup, and immediately the horses stopped except for that sidling movement that brought their hot, panting bodies closer in towards the Legionnaire. Tex looked up at the Arab who had dragged him along by the stirrup. He began to say, 'You fellars from Nuhas Pasha's army . . . ?'

A movement arrested the words, a movement from that Arab leaning down from his saddle before him. Tex saw a lean, sinewy, brown hand shoot down; agonized, felt those strong fingers grip his hair through his kepi. Out of the corner of his eye he caught a glint of metal reflecting, and though it nearly tore the hair out of his scalp, he managed to get his head round to see what it signified.

He saw an exultant Arab standing in his stirrups. He had his curved *flissa*, that razor-edged Arab sword, out and whistling round his head. Tex saw those intent, brown eyes, saw where they were looking.

They were on his neck, exposed and held for the blow by that pain-searing grip on his hair. In a second he'd have his head lopped off . . .

Tex's long leg kicked up. He didn't like to do it, but also he didn't want to have his head chopped off like any Christmas turkey's.

He booted that Arab horse in its stomach, and the animal whinnied, more with shock than actual pain, and immediately went rearing back on its hindlegs — so far back that it nearly toppled over. The Arab rider suddenly found a need for both hands if he were going to keep in the saddle and that meant releasing his grip on Tex's hair.

Tex promptly dropped to his knee, and the sword missed him by a good nine inches. But it had been near, too near for the American Legionnaire's liking.

His next move was instinctive. His left hand clawed downwards, gripped and lifted. A useless revolver came leaping up to cover those Arabs.

They weren't to know that it was useless from the mud and water that was in the action, however, and startled gasps testified to their shocked surprise. It was the second time that the Texan's quickness on the draw had turned the tables on his enemies that afternoon.

He shouted, 'Goldarn you, you treacherous apes what did you want to do that for? I thought you were friends . . . '

He had them covered, knew they were bluffed by that useless gun. He started to walk backwards, towards that broken sandstone wall. Still irate, still sore from that grip on his hair, he said again, 'Why did you do that?' only this time he remembered to speak in Legion Arabic.

One of the Arabs, he with the sword, watched him with glittering eyes. Then, for no reason at all, he answered and spoke the truth. 'It was the Sheik Mahmoud, our master's wish. He has sworn to wipe out all infidels, and he went against the wishes of Nuhas Pasha and sent us after you.'

Tex said, 'He's a nice guy, that Mahmoud,' and knew without being told which of those sheiks he had left that previous day was the man in question. That would be the sullen-eyed one, the thin-faced hombre with the look of an angry rattlesnake.

Tex was going backwards. Then the Arab shouted, 'We die unless we take your head!' And then, because he was a bold man, he drove his horse forward to stamp down the Americano.

Tex just turned and ran. His guns were useless until he could clean them, and he wasn't risking an explosion in the barrel by pulling trigger with all that dirt down the rifling. He jumped into a fissure that cleft the sandstone face. It ascended steeply and zig-zagged, and was evidently a drain poured by water running from off the top of the rock. It was rough going, but no horse could follow up it.

Tex climbed like lightning. He heard fierce, shouting voices, and without looking round guessed that the Arabs had dismounted and were coming after him. He found his way blocked by a big boulder. Dragging himself over it, he felt a movement.

He put his shoulder to it and kept rocking it, the while he heard voices coming nearer. Then the Arabs must have seen the rocking stone that could only tumble down the fissure in which they were climbing, and they turned and fled before it as fast as any mountain goats.

They were probably down that fissure before the boulder started rolling — were on their horses before it came crashing on to the desert in a flurry of sharp stone splinters and dust. Then they saw something else which decided their next course of action, and they put spurs to their mounts and went high-tailing it southwards as fast as they could go.

Tex clambered up the gulley until it began to split into a number of smaller channels. He had a feeling, even then, that the fissure made a good pathway towards the top of the rock . . .

And then he found that he couldn't go any further — not without great difficulty, anyway. Here the top of the rock was eroded, where a broad sheet of water swept over in the heavy winter rains that could turn this desert into a quagmire within a matter of minutes. But there was little in the way of assistance for climbing — no convenient gulley, anyway — and if he sought to go higher it would only bring him into view of the Arabs, whom he thought to be still below, on the broad face of the rock.

Tex sat down to recover his breath. He needed a halt. That chase across the desert had been heavy going; then that mad gallop, attached to the stirrup of a racing horse, had taken all the wind out of his bellows. Now this — a hard climb up a rainwater channel in rough sandstone. He'd certainly taken enough exercise for one day!

He looked at the yellow-red eye that was the sun, just beginning to dip below the horizon. He thought, 'I've got to get a hoss.' A man without a horse in this desert was a man near to losing his life. He couldn't exist without horseflesh . . .

He saw a billowing cloud of dust approaching from the direction of the oasis, half a mile away. He wiped the sweat from his eyes and watched. Saw blue under flying Arab cloaks and knew them to be three of the renegades. He was beginning to understand now why they so badly wanted to kill him.

'I saw what they did at El Kwatra,' he

thought. 'If I live, some day I might talk an' get them shot for what they did.'

When he turned his head he saw the three Arabs who had wanted his head for that fierce sheik, Mahmoud, racing away southwards. He had a feeling he would meet them again. They wouldn't dare go back to their master empty-handed. 'Kill that Legionnaire,' Mahmoud had said, and the Arabs would go to the ends of the earth to obey their dreaded master.

Tex shrugged. He'd just got rid of three enemies, when another three hove in sight.

Worse, he suddenly realized, they must have seen him, sitting high up there in that rainwater gulley. And they had Lebels. They needn't come up after him, risking boulders; they could watch from below and shoot him down.

He looked round for cover. It wasn't much good going back to where the gulley was deeper, giving some cover from the desert, because if the renegades remembered their Legionnaire training they would leave one man out in the desert to give covering fire, while the other two crept up and routed him out.

There were plenty of holes in the rock into which he could crawl, he realized. Just at this point where he was sitting the whole face of the sandstone cliff was honeycombed with caves He tried to think where he had seen such an effect before, and remembered it was on the Rio Grande where cave-dwelling Indians still lived in the rocks.

He began to crawl towards a near one, changed his mind and headed for one more remote up the cliffside. The renegades were still some distance off, perhaps the better part of a quarter of a mile. They wouldn't be able to spot which hole he had gone into, and if he could only escape detection for half an hour, darkness would be there to screen him.

Tex slipped into the cave. He lay on his stomach at the entrance, for a few moments watching the oncoming horsemen. He saw them halt, right below him. They were Cheauvin the Weeper, Mervin Petrie, late guillotine assistant, and the Bulgar.

They looked up at the cliff before

them, and had a short conference. They knew the Legionnaire Texas was somewhere up on this cliffside, because they had seen his blue tunic plainly from a distance. But where was he now? That was puzzling, for they could see no sign of the big, rangy Legionnaire.

Just as Tex had anticipated, the party split up. The Bulgar, who was quite a marksman, stood down on the desert, rifle held at the ready. Cheauvin the Belgian, and the Frenchman Mervin Petrie, gingerly started towards the rainwater gulley.

Tex sat back, away from the entrance, and took out his revolver. He laid the ammunition in neat rows to catch the last hot rays of the dying sun. In this arid atmosphere they would quickly dry out and would probably be unimpaired by the immersion . . . probably weren't even now, because they hadn't been under water for long, but still, best to dry them out.

The real bother was the gun. His holster had caught the mud and there was plenty caking the revolver. If those Arabs hadn't been so startled, they might have noticed that and drawn a few conclusions.

Hastily he took it to pieces and began to clean it on his shirt. A sound made him stop. He looked out, but the approaching Legionnaires weren't in sight. He frowned. That sound had seemed very near to him.

Hastily he began to assemble the revolver. When it was done he tested the action and it worked all right. He loaded the revolver, and immediately set to work cleaning his Lebel. That was a bigger job. He would need this rifle if he were to shoot his way out of a tight corner later. A revolver was good only for close quarter work and in desert strategy there wasn't much of that. A rifle demanded a rifle as a counter weapon.

But it took time. He didn't get it cleaned and assembled before he heard Petrie's voice outside. Petrie was shouting down to the Bulgar, eighty feet below.

'Watch out *mon ami*. The fox has gone to ground in one of these so-many caves. We will dig him out . . . '

But there were a lot of caves, and the

sun was almost extinguished. They would have to move fast if they were to find him before it became too dark to see.

He worked frantically on his rifle, listening to the sounds of search. They had begun their search much too close to Tex's hideout, for his satisfaction. He thought of jumping out of the cave and blazing away with his revolver, but he knew that would probably bring an instant stream of lead from the Bulgar below, and he restrained the impulse. But if one of them came to the cave entrance . . .

He heard the Weeper's voice — Cheauvin the Belgian's. It seemed to be almost at the entrance to this cave that he was in. He put down his rifle, nearly assembled again, and turned to pick up his revolver. Caught a movement from the blackness behind him.

A slim, brown hand was just reaching down. He saw the fingers grab the revolver and begin to lift it . . . realized this was no gunnery expert, for the fingers hadn't closed automatically around the trigger as usually happened.

Frantically Tex dived, rolling in mid-air as he did so. He caught that slim wrist, and rolled his weight up the bare arm. He heard a body crash into the sand with a thud; there was a gasp of pain, and the fight went out of that arm. Tex grabbed the revolver and scuttled back to the cave entrance. Peeping out, he looked on to Cheauvin's head. Cheauvin was entering a cave about fifteen feet below.

Tex realized that night was coming fast; it was almost dark. Here in the Sahara night followed day with almost miraculous swiftness — one moment it was light, the next almost complete darkness.

Mervin Petrie must have realized how close to night they were, too, for suddenly Tex heard his rough voice grumbling, '*Mon ami*, we shall assuredly fall and break our precious necks if we do not get down that steep waterway before darkness. Let us return to the oasis, and leave the accursed pig-dog of an Americano to freeze in his hole.'

Cheauvin was quick to agree. He hadn't enjoyed searching these dark caves, anyway. It was all right for Petrie and the Bulgar to argue, 'He is out of ammunition. See, though he has guns, he does not use them. Assuredly they are harmless, then.'

Sound reasoning, but the Belgian wasn't so sure of it, all the same.

Tex relaxed with a sigh of relief as he heard those stumbling footsteps down the fissure — and the curses as they bruised themselves on the rough rocks. So long as they cleared off, night or no night he'd find his way down to the desert again.

And then what? He shrugged. Back to that oasis where his enemies were, in the hope of finding his horse — his or anyone else's. Hastily he finished assembling his rifle. Soon he might need it.

Then he went back to see his opponent who would have stolen his gun from him.

It was a girl.

It came as a shock to Tex to know that he had knocked out a girl in the struggle for that gun. Inadvertently, of course, yet effectively. Hastily he dragged her towards the entrance of the cave, so that he could see her by the last of the day's light. Down below he heard men's gruff voices speaking together, then the jingle of bridle bits and the creak of saddle leather. And then the muffled thud of horse's hooves as the men rode away.

The girl was an Arab. She was of the *fellahin* class too — a simple, peasant girl by the look of her crude, homespun, cotton dress. She had good features, though, as so many of these Arab girls away from the towns possessed, and her hair was richly black and luxuriant.

Tex, staring down, wondering what next to do, suddenly realized that the eyes were slightly open — realized that the girl wasn't knocked out at all, but playing possum. No doubt she had hoped it would save her — or maybe give her the opportunity of seizing his revolver a second time.

He thought, 'One second more and this beauty sure would have blown my brains out!'

He found himself drawling, 'You can quit your shamming, sister.' Then sought for words in Arabic. 'You needn't worry. I won't harm you.'

She sat up at that and crouched back

against the wall, plainly not at all reassured by his words. He saw big, almost black eyes fixed upon him, and he realized that in them was less terror than hatred. This girl would turn the tables on him if she had half a chance.

He demanded, 'What're you doing here?' Yet he knew the answer almost as soon as he asked the question. This big rock would be a good watch-post, from which the former inhabitants could keep their oasis under observation. No doubt this girl had been left on watch, to report on events since the departure of the tribe. That meant, he realized, that the Arab women and children and their flocks and herds must be fairly close, hiding out in some desert valley nearby.

The girl never answered, just looked sullenly at him, crouching back against that wall of rock. So Tex shrugged. He went out of the cave almost as the last rays of light fell on them. He wanted to get down the tricky cliffside, but with the passing of light he knew it was suicide to attempt it. He remembered there was a moon that night, though it came up after midnight, and philosophically he decided to wait for it to rise.

He went back into the cave, put his rifle up against the wall behind him, and then stretched himself on the sandy cave bottom. The sand was hot and soft and made a comfortable bed for the Legionnaire. He sighed, suddenly realizing how tired he was. A few hours' sleep would do him a mighty lot of good.

He could see the vague outline of the Arab girl, but he had no fear of her. He told her he was going to sleep until the moon rose, when he would attempt to get down that awkward rain gully. She didn't move, didn't seem to relax at his words — probably didn't believe him, because no Arab believed that a Legionnaire was without harm.

Yet he slept for four hours, until his trained instincts brought him awake as the silvery moon began to lift over the desert. He sat up, enjoying the freshness of the night air. It was cool, but not one of those cold nights which sometimes hit the desert even in mid-summer.

The girl stirred at his movement, then

quickly jerked herself erect. She had finally lain down and gone to sleep. Now he caught the flash of her eyes in the moonlight. She was still filled with suspicion, still watching him.

He ignored her. She could look after herself, otherwise she wouldn't have been left here on watch by her people. His thoughts were on the task ahead.

First, descent from the rock. Then find a horse. And then . . . ? Then find ex-Nazi General Sturmer, captain in the French Foreign Legion. Find Sturmer — but don't let the *partizan* leader find him!

When the moon was high enough, Tex stepped out of the cave and began to descend that treacherous pathway. He was pretty sure that no enemies lurked in wait for him at the foot, because that silvery moon gave enough light to see even as far as the oasis.

The girl he simply ignored. That was the best way to treat these primitive Arab tribeswomen. The more you spoke to them, even to tell them you meant no harm, the more they distrusted you and were ready for anything — including eye-scratching attacks and hysterical scream-ing. Tex wanted neither.

After he had gone down the gully a short distance, however, he heard stum-bling footsteps behind him, and a whimper of fear. He didn't know then that the girl should have returned to her people while it was still daylight, but had been prevented by the arrival of Arabs and Legionnaires. And she was as superstitious as any of her kind, and to her the night was filled with evil spirits. Even the cursed infidel was preferable to being alone.

She was barefooted, and winced and cried out several times as she hurt her feet on the moonlit, rocky pathway. Tex found himself distancing her, and she must have panicked, for suddenly he heard a tremulous call, 'O thou son of France, help a poor unfortunate girl on to the desert where I can walk to safety.'

Tex sighed, but couldn't ignore that frightened appeal. He waited, and she came up to him, then he helped her down over the hard parts.

Near to the bottom, though, he made

her fend for herself. When he came out into the open he wanted both hands free in case of ambush.

None came, however.

Tex immediately started to walk westwards, towards where he knew the oasis to be. When he breasted a small hill, he saw the dark, shadowy shape of the trees ahead of him.

He also realized that the Arab girl was running after him. She was terrified of being out alone on this desert. Did not her people speak of a devil in the form of a great writhing worm that scoured the sands at night and ate up every living thing so that the desert might be clean and undefiled next day? And wasn't there a half-man, half-crocodile who lived in the shadows and snapped up night-walkers between teeth that were so poisoned by an evil breath that was also to be found in the marshes?

He stopped and turned, his shadow long in the moonlight. He was perplexed, This sure gummed things up. He couldn't have an Ay-rab girl following where he intended to go!

The girl went down on her knees pleadingly before the big ex-cowpuncher. In melting, tearful Arabic she begged him not to leave her to the evil denizens of the desert night. He looked down into a face that was filled with terror, and in that bright moonlight she looked lovely — her hair was lustrous, her eyes bigger than he had ever seen eyes before and brown and soft. He saw the shadows on her face, that threw her cheekbones into prominence . . . She looked different . . . Oriental . . . appealing.

He said, 'The hell, you can't come with me,' and started to stride off towards that oasis once more.

But she did. Suddenly he felt a grip on his arm and turned and saw the girl trotting by his side. She was hanging on to him, her fear gone of the infidel, taking no chances of being left alone in the desert.

He stopped and disengaged himself again. Spoke patiently to her. 'My sister,' he said in fairly good Arabic, 'where I go is no place for a girl. Go thou and find the people. There is nothing to harm you in this desert except man.'

But she wouldn't believe him. When he moved again, she clung close to him.

He sighed. 'Sometimes I sure would be flattered to be needed by a brunette as lovely as you, honey! But not now!' She looked at him, but didn't understand a word of that drawling Texan voice

He pushed her away yet again, and walked quickly onwards. She was by his side in an instant. There was no losing her.

So, because there was no alternative, he took her with him.

It still didn't deter him from the task ahead. First, find a horse.

It was eerie work, plunging into the gloom of those trees that ringed the oasis — even eerier was that last minute or so of tramping across open desert towards silent bushes, which might contain an enemy.

But they didn't. With a sigh of relief Tex decided that he hadn't been expected to come back, and no one was keeping watch for him.

Silently, like a big shadow, he moved

among the trees, avoiding always the open, cultivated fields over which he had stumbled only a few hours before. The girl moved silently with him, sensing the need for caution, and in fact was no hindrance to his movements.

He worked round the village, distinguishable by its stink in the shadows under those palm trees, until he had almost encircled the oasis. There was no sign of a horse wandering loose, yet he knew his own wouldn't have run into the desert. No animal ever left water and vegetation unless compelled to do so.

After a time he decided that the renegades must have captured his mount and brought it into the village with their own. He sat down then, against a clump of coarse, broad-leaved grasses that were almost twice the height of a man in places, and tried to work things out. The girl came and sat very close to him. She'd even forgotten he was an infidel, and therefore had the evil eye. All she knew was that he hadn't harmed her, didn't seem even interested in her — and he was one good looking piece of man!

Tex thought of his horse. Could be they'd captured it so that he couldn't use it to make a getaway from the vicinity of that water hole. Could be they knew he must have a horse and would come looking for it, even into the village, and they were using it as bait in the hope of trapping him. That would explain why there had been no warning shout when he stumbled out of the desert a bare half-hour earlier — keeping watch all around the perimeter of an oasis was a big job, requiring all of them to be on guard. But keeping watch on a horse in the centre of a native village was easier — one man at a time only need lie and cover the place with his rifle.

Tex thought, 'They know that Mahomet's got to go to the mountain.'

But he had no alternative. If he didn't get a horse, so that he could ride away from that deathtrap of an oasis, they would rout him out the next day and despatch him. He was armed now, but one armed man couldn't turn the tables on six desperadoes. For none of the men was a coward, unless he excepted the

Belgian, Cheauvin.

He told the girl what he was going to do. Told her about the horse and the danger that would come to him when he tried to get it.

But when he rose and began to go to where he knew the village to lie, the girl went with him. She was his shadow for the rest of that night, and now he knew it and gave up trying to turn her away. He'd just have to try to keep her from getting hurt, that was all.

They had taken about twenty strides, and were still in the thorn scrub around the edge of the cultivated area, when all in one second night dissolved and there was full, blinding daylight.

Everywhere around them, men rose out of the ground and began to walk forward.

4

Tex hurled the Arab maiden to the ground, and fell beside her. She rolled up against him and clung to his shoulder, terrified.

Tex lifted his head, cautiously, looking across and not directly into that brilliant light. He knew it was a searchlight, mounted on top of a patrol vehicle. Those men who had come tramping in from the desert were soldiers — probably Legionnaires.

Crouching low, covered by a prickly-pear bush, he saw the crescent of men come advancing cautiously in among the bushes, heard the crash of heavy feet on dried vegetation. The advancing men carried their rifles against their hips, ready for instant action.

They were coming straight towards where Tex and the Arab girl lay.

Then he looked beyond, on to the bare, moonlit desert through the thin fringe of the palm trees. He saw a line of horsemen silently waiting, saw Arab burnouses and knew them at once.

These, because they were co-operating with French troops, must be the dreaded *partizans*, renegade Arab hunters of Legion deserters. If that were so, he thought, then he'd better keep right out of sight, for his enemy, Herman Sturmer, would be with them.

His pulse raced at the thought that he might be near to his enemy. If only he could get the chance to seize him again, render him helpless . . . then somehow he'd get him to the Oasis Bir Khula, where he had friends who would help him to get the war criminal out of the country.

First, though, evade detection by this advancing column of soldiers.

He saw one man silhouetted for an instant against the white glare of that blinding white searchlight. He was a Legionnaire.

Instantly Tex whispered to the girl and shoved her under the prickly-pear bush. She winced, testifying to the sharpness of those inch-long spikes on the big flat leaves, but did as she was told.

Tex instantly unslung his rifle and dropped it against his thigh, just like the advancing men. Then, a few seconds before the line of advancing, unspeaking soldiers reached him, he stood erect by that bush.

His ruse worked. Rising as he did, almost in line with the Legionnaires, they took him to be one of themselves. Tex stood for a few seconds, as if examining that dense clump of bushes; the Legionnaires divided on either side of him, and passed the girl and she was safe.

Tex breathed a sigh of relief. For a few strides he pretended to keep up with the men, in case anyone was watching in the rear, by that powerful light. Then he fell on his knees suddenly, so that he was below the level of that streaming searchlight, and began to work his way back to where the girl lay.

She was shaking with fright when he put his hand on her, then she must have recognized him in the dark, and he felt warm hands grasp his as if she would never let go.

He whispered, 'Lie still,' and crouched down beside her. He was watching Sturmer's *partizans*, out there in the desert . . .

Distantly came the thud of racing hooves. Horsemen were spurring away to the south of the oasis. A shout came from the line of Legionnaires — 'Arabs!' Then one or two shots rang out, as if someone hopefully took a pot at receding horsemen.

After that there was quite a lot of shouting from the men, each shout more reassuring than the last. Listening, Tex got the whole story. Six Arabs had bolted from the village on their horses. Now the village was deserted — was safe, *mon officier*, to occupy the place. Only, Tex knew that they weren't Arabs who had bolted. That would be Ca-ca and his renegades, fleeing in disguise. Evidently they had no wish to rejoin the Legion yet.

Tex thought, 'There goes my hoss, too.' It was no good trying to find a mount down in the village now.

The *partizans* hadn't moved from their position on the edge of the desert.

Probably they were being used as cavalry, to move where directed in case of Arab attack. But that was no use to Tex, crouching there and watching those hooded figures sitting out there in the full radiance of the silent, streaming moonlight.

He couldn't stay inside that oasis till morning light. He must be away into the desert before dawn. Because with light would come recognition, either from Sturmer or from sharp-eyed *partizans*, who had no cause to like the Texan.

But where could he go into the desert? Without horse and food and water, that great Sahara was just a deathtrap for him when the sun rose . . .

The Arab girl was whispering, 'Come. We go to my people. They will not hurt you.' Her eyes were shining. She was beginning to get ideas about this big Legionnaire.

Tex nodded. It was worth trying. Anyway, what was the alternative?

He began to crawl through the undergrowth, the girl following. Twice they had to go to ground — once when a

Legionnaire came blundering back towards that light, as if to make a report, the other time, shortly afterwards, when a party of officers walked through towards the Arab village.

In time, however, they reached the last bushes on the edge of that great, rolling desert that looked so white and beautiful in the moonlight and gave no hint of its cruelty by day.

There they had to stop. The nearest *partizans*, true, were a good eighty yards away, but Tex knew that if they tried to cross that open waste, they would be detected immediately. He had no wish to be detected. He knew his head would come off if he were recognized, for to some of the *partizans* he was known to be a deserter, and that was the *partizan* treatment of a man 'on pump'.

They lay, crouched in the shadow of some tall, coarse grasses, waiting and watching for a chance to break out of the oasis. Then, quite suddenly, the *partizans* began to move around, until they assumed some formation, and then they began to walk their horses southwards.

That would bring them past Tex and the girl. Tex suddenly cursed and wished he had hidden up deeper in the oasis. But it was too late now to move . . .

He pulled the girl's head down against his tunic, and lay with face averted himself, because he knew that eyes caught light and could produce betraying gleams.

He heard the clop-clop of hooves until they were almost level with him, and then he was unable to resist the temptation to look up.

He did, shooting a quick glance from under his tunic sleeve,

He looked straight into the thin, sallow, beglassed face of Captain Sturmer, late general in the German African army.

Sturmer was riding at the head of his men, his face peering into the shadows. He was in his usual get-up, a Legion captain's uniform except for the Arab headdress in place of a kepi.

For one awful second it seemed to Tex that the captain was looking straight at him where he lay with the girl; then the face turned away with a flash of eyeglasses, and Tex knew he was safe.

In a matter of seconds the cavalcade was out of sight, following a pathway through the oasis to the village. When he considered it safe, Tex rose, took the girl by the hand and started to run towards that distant outcrop of crumbling sandstone. When they had gone a few hundred yards in the desert, the girl began to take the lead. She was on familiar country.

She spoke, when it seemed safe and their voices wouldn't reach hostile ears. Her people were in a basin in which was a small spring some leagues behind that big sandstone rock. They would be worrying, because she had been left to keep watch on the six strangers who had entered their village and failed to return.

At length when they had skirted the sandstone and were half an hour's walk beyond it, the girl said they were quite near to the hideout of the tribe. Tex even thought he heard distant sounds of sheep and cattle. At that he halted and told the girl he would stay where he was until the sun rose. He wanted full light before he met whatever dangers this village held for him.

He lowered himself to the ground. There was no discomfort in sleeping anywhere — one patch of sand made as good a bed as the next in this desert, and the night was warm and he didn't need a blanket. Sometimes, of course, it grew chilly, but this wasn't one of those nights.

The girl came and sat by him. He watched her, quite clearly revealed by that brilliant moon. She looked soft and round-cheeked and lovely. Tex closed his eyes. He wanted sleep.

He felt the girl come closer, then she took his hand in hers. He opened one eye. She was smiling so sweetly down at him.

The Texan patted her hand. 'Baby, you're gettin' ideas to that pretty head, ain't you?' She looked puzzled at this drawling, foreign language. So he sought out his Arabic again. 'Sleep, my child. I have many wives and I wish to dream of them.'

The girl said, 'Oh!' and looked petulant, then lay down couple of yards from him and curled up, and he never heard from her till morning.

He closed that one eye. *L'amour* was

all very well, but he didn't want complications with this girl when he reached her tribe.

The first reflecting rays of sunshine brought them to their feet even before the crescent rim lifted above the eastern sandhills. The girl had recovered her temper and smiled sweetly at him. He took her hand. Holding a hand as pretty as that was no hardship, and he didn't think it would get complicated.

The Arab girl smiled and held on. It wasn't every day she met such a fine-looking man as this big, drawling-voiced Legionnaire. She kept looking at him, and dropping her soft lashes, and then lifting them and beaming. After a while she even began to blush when she met his eyes, a lovely dusky red under the smooth brownness of her cheeks.

Tex thought, 'Uh, uh! She's gettin' ideas again in spite of my many wives.' He decided that holding hands might be complicating, after all, but he couldn't get his hand away when he tried. Not tactfully, that is. The gal sure was a clinger.

Suddenly they came upon her people. They had ascended a hill from which protruded a scattered array of rocks, like a mass of broken teeth, and were able to look down into a shallow pocket in the desert. In the centre was a flush of green, with even a few small bushes growing, testifying to the presence of water. But there were no trees.

Trying to find sustenance on that thin crop of grass were a few hundred sheep, goats, cattle, camels and horses. In a huddle to one side, so that they would not cover the precious vegetation, were a lot of black tents, irregular in shape, as was the Arab way.

People were stirring when the Arab girl and Tex came walking up to the tents. A few were returning with pitchers on their heads from a tiny spring in the centre of the hollow. Tex knew of these small seep-holes in the desert. Generally they dried up in the late summer, and for that reason did not support life such as trees ... for that reason, too, no permanent villages were set up around them. All the same, as a temporary refuge for themselves and their precious flocks, this tiny spring was invaluable to the tribe at this moment.

The girl had released Tex's hand, so that she would not be seen on such intimate terms with the infidel. She walked slightly ahead of the Westerner, and he could feel a nervousness developing in her bearing; she knew she was in for a storm of criticism.

She got it. People began to call and get excited as they were seen. As they reached the nearest tents, a crowd had gathered to receive them. It wasn't a silent crowd. In rising tones of anger and fear, they shouted questions at the approaching girl, and she was so intimidated that she shrank back against the long-striding Legionnaire.

Tex halted and looked at those people. Mostly they were women and children, but with a few infirm old men tottering in their midst. All who could ride a horse would be away at the fighting, of course.

That made him glance across towards the horses. Usually they took all the good beasts with them. He could only see a

couple that weren't old and broken, left
here in the charge of these women, and
they weren't anything to shout about, his
critical glance told him.

He looked back at those drab-costumed
women, with their brown wrinkled faces,
and bright angry eyes. He got the drift of
what they were shouting, though the dia-
lect was hard to follow.

Where had she been, stopping out all
night? Tex found humour in the question.
Wasn't that what every mother asked her
daughter, all the world over?

But the other questions were without
humour. Who was this infidel, and was
she mad to bring their enemies right into
their secret retreat?

They began to crowd forward, and the
girl was terrified. She wheeled suddenly
on Tex, her confidence lost. He saw eyes
open in fear, saw the pleading in them to
be saved from the wrath of her kinsfolk.
In the night the proposition hadn't
seemed so bad. She would go to her
people and explain the kindness of this
Legionnaire, and how he had looked after
her and done her no harm. But now,

confronting them, in the fierce brightness of the day, she knew she had miscalculated. They weren't to be appeased and made agreeable by easy talk.

Tex saw her mouth opening and closing, as if trying to say things and yet unable to find words. He put his hand on her shoulder to comfort her and bring her strength. Somewhere someone started to scream. He had a feeling it wasn't a woman, either.

He removed his hand from the girl's shoulder and lifted it, and intoned the customary Arab greeting, 'Allah be with you!'

The crowd went silent at that, facing him with hostility. Tex called out that he was a friend, that he was no longer a Legionnaire, and then as an afterthought he added that Nuhas Pasha the Great had said his life should be spared.

It cut no ice. That crowd either didn't know anything about Nuhas Pasha, because they were women and weren't permitted into the conversation of men, or they didn't believe his story, anyway. He wore the uniform of their tyrannical masters, and they knew only one treatment for such mercenaries.

Death.

. . . or perhaps two treatments. Torture first, and then death. But always death, in the end. As with that other Legionnaire who had come stumbling in upon them the previous evening. He had received half of the treatment only . . .

Tex heard that moaning, screaming voice again. It was quite near. It made shudders run down his spine, but he daren't lift his eyes because this mob, for all there were few men in it, was threatening.

They were coming closer. They were shouting more angrily. There was a savagery in the air, a sudden wildness that spoke of brutal deeds to follow. The women were working themselves up into a fury of excitement, and their target was as much this girl as the big Legionnaire who had walked in with her.

She was scared out of her wits, turning now to the infidel in panic. He had to push her away, because she was sobbing and clinging to him, completely losing her head.

Tex shouted, 'Shut up, shut up! Let me speak. This girl is not at fault!' But they were past shutting up; they wanted to vent their anger on them and nothing was going to stop them, or so they shouted in return.

The truth was, life was very hard for these women, without their menfolk and away from the shade of the oasis. Stuck out in the desert by this feeble, dying spring, was no life for them, especially for the ones with children. So now they felt like dissipating some of their anger and frustration upon the tall Legionnaire — and also upon the fool of a girl who had brought him in with her.

She was a little fool, of course, they argued. She should know these fickle, faithless, treacherous Franks by now, and not be taken in by their soft tongues. No doubt this tall son of a pig had made love to her, for the purpose of finding the hiding place of the missing tribe. But if he thought to talk sweetly to them and be allowed to go away and tell his comrades and then bring them back on an expedition of loot and slaughter, he was mistaken.

All this they told the girl, and told Tex, too. Tex gripped his Lebel tighter and thought, 'There ain't no hoss comin' outa this crowd — not unless I take it!'

He also thought, 'I couldn't use this blamed gun on a passel o' women.'

But when they came surging forward, suddenly, violently, he lifted his Lebel, all the same, and covered the leaders. They were fat Arab women, and they must have felt that at that range not even a blind man could have missed them, so they just as suddenly came to a stop.

Sight of that menacing rifle shut their voices, too. Back of the crowd some of the old men tried to find guns, but all that were any use had been taken by their menfolk. Knives and sticks, that's all they had against that rifle.

Tex put on a show of authority. 'Stand back, gals.' His gun waved. They needed no translation and fell back. That scream suddenly welled up again. Tex stiffened. He thought he distinguished a word in that trailing moan of high-pitched sound. He wanted to turn his head, but still daren't.

In Arabic he told them, 'I am no enemy of your people. I like not the ways of your French masters and will no longer fight with them. But I must have a horse to get away from them. See, I have some money. I will buy a horse from you.'

And the money he showed were some precious American dollars that he had saved against emergency while in the Legion.

It didn't move them. They wanted his life; after that they could help themselves to his money. They were a pretty logical crowd, those Arab women staring at the fluttering dollar notes.

The girl said something. She tried to say it without moving her lips, without turning her head, so that the crowd wouldn't know she was warning the Legionnaire. He got the words: 'Do not trust them. They are evil and will kill you.'

He thought, 'Thanks, baby. Just what I was thinking.' He knelt and put a couple of five dollar bills under a stone. That was the price of a horse hereabouts, he thought. Then he began to retreat towards the horses, his Lebel covering that crowd.

This time the girl didn't follow him.

Tex saw she was crying. Big tears were rolling down that pretty face. She must have known she couldn't go with him, and besides fear there was regret on her face. To this simple Arab maiden, the big Texan was like a god, a man above other men she had known.

Tex went back towards those grazing horses. One had a headrope trailing, as if it had been ridden perhaps on watch overnight. Perhaps for that reason it didn't start to walk nervously away with the other horses, because it was tired and didn't expect further work. Tired . . . but a horse, and that was all he wanted.

He was very close to it when he heard that despairing moan again. This time he glanced towards the end tent, from whence the sound came. Or rather, he saw, from just outside it

Someone appeared to be lying under a blue blanket on the ground before the black tent, was his first impression. As he quickly dragged his eyes back, latent impression told him it was a man, and he wasn't lying voluntarily there. He had caught the hint of pegs . . . that body was spreadeagled, staked out to the ground.

With a stir of excitement he realized something else. That 'blanket' was the blue tunic of a Legionnaire . . .

That moan came again — 'Tex! Tex!' And this time, 'Oh, god, help me, Tex! These fiends . . . '

He caught the headrope and pulled a surprised horse towards him. Without mounting he began to walk across to the spreadeagled Legionnaire. He'd be some unfortunate deserter, he thought, some-one going on pump only to be captured and tortured by these fierce women.

The crowd was shouting and screaming abuse at him, raging at the possibility of losing their victim. Tex looked as savage as he could and swung that rifle, and though they kept on clamouring, none came forward in the face of that threat.

So, towing the reluctant horse behind him, Tex at length came and stood over that pain-wracked figure. He looked down on to the disorderliness of open tunic and coarse torn shirt. Saw a face as scrub-coloured as his own.

Recognized those fever-bright brown eyes, those ugly yellow, protruding teeth.

'Louie!' he gasped, and then his face went hard. For Louie, an American Legionnaire, had once betrayed him and his comrades to the enemy, Captain Herman Sturmer and his head-hunting *partizans*.

5

Louie looked up at him and moaned. 'Tex, get me outa here; Oh, god, Tex, the things they've done to me . . . ' And then, eyes narrowing with pain, he whimpered, 'I'm sorry, Tex, for what I did. I guess I'm a goddamned coward. I should never have come into this place. I haven't got the sand . . . '

Tex said, 'Forget it, Louie.'

Almost his last words to his former comrade had been, 'You'd better keep outa my way from now on, Louie.' That was when they were under fire, and Louie was across with their enemies.

Tex stood on the headrope — he wasn't going to risk losing his mount now. He stooped, watching that crowd now. Thank heaven they hadn't a gun between them: this Lebel made him master of the situation. But if any Arab men came riding back to their womenfolk . . .

Swiftly he cut through the bonds.

Groaning, Louie tried to sit up but failed. Tex put his arm round him and aided him. Somehow Louie got to his feet. He was very ill. He kept moaning, 'The things they did to me, them women. They ain't human.'

Tex said, 'They've suffered a lot, Louie. They feel they've a lot of scores to settle.' Then he asked, 'Can you ride a hoss?'

Louie's ugly face went grim. 'I'd ride a tiger if it could get me outa this hell hole.'

So Tex gave him his precious Lebel. 'You cover them critters while I round up another cayuse.'

He saw the quick, eager way that Louie grasped the gun, saw the light of ferocity in those brown, pain-ridden eyes, and his own face went hard and merciless. He understood what was going on in the tortured Legionnaire's mind and he gave a blunt warning.

'You use that gun as a threat, Louie. Don't you go findin' excuses fer firin' it, savvy? If you kill one o' the women, as sure as there's sand on this desert, I'll pump a hole through your ugly head.'

Louie looked at him and quailed before

the grim-faced Texan. He mumbled, 'I wasn't thinkin' of anythin' like that Tex. You know me, don't you?' — pathetically. But all the same Tex knew he had read those thoughts correctly. He'd seen the joy in that face, seen the way his eyes had blazed in triumph towards some of those fat old women.

But Louie wouldn't dare start anything now. Louie's life wasn't worth any more than any of these people's here.

He swung astride that bare-backed Arab pony. He wasn't concerned about being without saddle and with only a single headrope. He'd been brought up to the Indian way of horse riding, and this was no different.

He rode round among the sheep and cattle, seeking a suitable horse for Louie. He picked out the best, an old beast but still with plenty of slow miles in him, caught him and got his belt round his neck and walked him back towards the tents. The women were becoming shriller again at the sight of a second horse being taken by these accursed Legionnaires, but they were helpless in the face of that rifle.

Louie held both mounts while Tex strode through the tents and found saddles and bridles, food and drink. He thought, 'We might just as well do the thing in style . . . '

He left more dollars. These people couldn't afford to lose precious property. Besides, he had all the dollars he needed back in the States.

Louie had to be helped up, but once in the saddle he sat his horse firmly enough. He kept looking at Tex, and once he muttered, 'The hell, Tex, I'm a heel an' I don't deserve it.'

The Texan said, 'We all do things we don't like to remember, Louie. Sometimes, I guess, life gets a bit too hard for us an' we lose our heads. I figger you did what you did because you were scared to death.' He swung into his saddle. 'I couldn't leave a man to torment and death, Louie, no matter what he'd done agen me.'

Louie started to thank him, started to say he was the finest man in the world, but it jarred on the Texan and quite roughly he told him to shut his mouth.

Then he began to walk his mount out past the Arabs, towards the open desert over the jagged-toothed rocks on the southern skyline.

The women weren't making much noise now. Perhaps they were relieved to see them go, after all, and the money that had been left spoke of good intentions, and no longer were they afraid of betrayal. All the same, a few would have liked to have finished that torture . . .

Louie said, 'When I got in among the *partizans*, I knew at once I'd made a mistake.' That was when Louie had turned traitor on his comrades; to save his life he had gone over to the enemy and left his Legionnaire friends — and a girl — in the lurch. Now he was saying it had all been a mistake.

'I got a feelin' as soon as them buzzards came crowdin' round me that nothin' would satisfy 'em but my head. I'd jumped from the fryin' pan into the fire.'

Tex was listening, but his eyes were on that group, on that lonely Arab girl out there before those women. They wouldn't believe he hadn't made love to her, and women were jealous and vengeful and sought to hurt those who had had a love denied them. That was women the world over. Now he saw a movement as women came surging forward. Some laid hands on the girl.

He reined in his horse.

Louie was mumbling on, 'The hell, I beat it the moment I saw a chance. They weren't expectin' me to bolt, I guess, not after I'd just thrown in with them. I kept ridin' north figgerin' on hittin' the coast or any place away from the awful desert. But I ran outa water, my hoss died under me an' I nearly passed out, too. Some old men found me in the desert when I was nearly a goner, an' they brought me here. They'd have been kinder to have left me to die of thirst, I reckon. You don't know what they did to me,' he ended again.

But Tex was staring back at that crowd of fierce women, aghast. They'd got the girl in their midst and were venting their anger and frustration upon her. They were behaving like any mob, cruelly, viciously, without heed to the rightness or consequences of what they were doing.

She was screaming with pain and terror. Someone had got her by that soft, gleaming-black hair that was probably her maidenly pride and was dragging her, for no reason except that it hurt, along before the tents.

Other screaming women were pummelling her and shouting abuse at this girl who had shown favour to an infidel. Hands lifted and fell with all the strength the owners could muster, hurting her; others were scratching, digging long nails deep into that soft flesh.

Tex thought, horrified, 'She might get killed — because of me!' There was no knowing what could happen when a mob lost its head like this.

The screams of the girl rose higher as the pain intensified. Tex thought, 'The hell, I can't go an' leave her like this.'

He had to do something. He did. He kicked his heels into his horse's ribs and raced back towards the crowd. They scattered in fear as they saw him return, all except a few vengeful women who retained their grip on the girl. They were fat and old and unlovely. There hadn't been a man in their lives for years, and they couldn't forgive this girl for having, as they thought, what would never be theirs.

Primitive, illogical, but that was how it was. They were giving her hell when Tex wheeled up on his horse.

He drew his revolver and brandished it with a great show of savagery. Even stood in his stirrups, as if to strike them down. And they fell before the threat, cowering and releasing their hold on the girl.

She fell to the ground, sobbing. Tex saw a tear-stained face, saw scratch marks disfiguring it. But he didn't dismount. He shouted to her, 'Get up. Get on to your feet!'

She rose at that, and stood swaying in the hot sand. Tex kicked his mount into action again — ran up beside the girl and stooped and caught her up beside him and then turned his horse and went racing away towards where Louie was waiting with the Lebel. The women cried out in consternation at that. The man with the evil eye was abducting one of their daughters.

One of their daughters was enjoying being abducted. Away from the camp, Tex looked at her as she clung to him, and he asked, 'Now, what do we do with you?'

Demurely she told him, 'Thou art my master. I go where thou goest.'

Tex said, irritably, 'I'm not your master. Look, have Louie, or find a nice quiet Arab husband who won't beat you more'n a couple of times a day.'

He was angry because he was in a jam. He knew it was too late. No nice young Arab would want a girl who had been seen publicly in the arms of an infidel, as she was just now. In saving her, she had become a lost woman, so far as her tribe was concerned. And that raised the problem — What was he going to do with her?

He growled, 'I get outa one jam an' go neck deep in another.'

But he couldn't leave the girl there to the mercy of those vicious women. He sighed and started his horse into a walk again, and Louie came riding up alongside him. Tex had provided himself with some goatskins of water, and now Louie lifted one and squirted a stream into his big mouth. He was feeling a lot better, though bruised and aching from the torment of the previous night.

The girl seemed suddenly quite at home. She wriggled on to the saddle before the big ex-cowboy, pushed back her hair and smiled engagingly with her big brown eyes at him. For a fallen woman she seemed remarkably cheerful.

Tex looked at her and growled. 'You minx.' Then he headed for the big sandstone rock from which a view of the oasis could be obtained. Captain Sturmer was there, the former Nazi general. Tex wasn't going to be turned from his purpose by anything, not even by the advent of this soft comely Arab maiden into his life.

It was complicating, that was all, but he'd find a way around the complications.

He talked with the girl, part of the way. What was she going to do? He couldn't trail her around with him. Did she think if she found her father and brothers they would listen to her and protect her when they took her back to the tribe?

Quite cheerfully the girl said she didn't want to find her people. Her menfolk would be as bad as her mother and those other spiteful women. No, she was quite content to be trailed around. She confided that the desert was a dreary place to live in, anyway.

Tex shelved the problem as the big rock pile loomed up. The future would dictate action with regard to the maiden.

By the cleft in the sandstone he halted their horses and dismounted. He led the beasts into the shadow of that gully and told the other two to stay there and wait.

Mahfra — he'd got her name by now; it meant 'Rain-in-Early-Summer' — shook her head. Where he went, she was going. Wasn't he her lord and master? But she was looking at the camel-faced Louie distrustfully. She had given her faith to one Legionnaire, and there wasn't any left over for another. This Lou-ee, he looked a poor type of man, her quick mind had decided.

Louie wasn't interested in anything except getting out of the saddle. Tex helped him down. When he touched the sand, Louie collapsed. Looking at that white, drawn face, Tex guessed at the things those women had done to him. Life must be hard for people to get so cruel, he thought.

He put the water skin beside the Legionnaire, told him he wouldn't be away long. Louie said, tiredly, 'You go, Tex. I'll be all right, I guess. All I want is rest.'

Tex nodded and started the climb. Mahfra came behind him for a while, then got impatient. She was as active as a goat and knew all the footholds. She skipped past Tex, her bare feet sure-footed where his big boots failed to grip. There were even times when she leaned back to help her lord and master.

The American accepted it resignedly. At last they came out where those caves, probably once used by the tribe's ancestors, marked the end of the way up. They sat back on the hot sloping rock, panting. Anyway, Tex was panting.

The sweat was in his eyes, and he removed his kepi. He squinted against the sun. Half a mile away was the oasis, very plain to their eyes in that blazing light. They saw the unmoving palms — even saw figures moving about among the trees. Tex hadn't realized how close they were, or else had forgotten, and now he hastily moved himself into a cave entrance. Outside, his blue tunic would show up to anyone looking their way.

For half an hour he watched, trying to formulate a plan of action. It was difficult to know what to do. Clearly it was useless just sitting here in the desert, for in a matter of hours their water would be gone, and they would want more food, anyway. Without much further loss of time they must strike out to some nearby oasis, otherwise they would soon die.

Tex considered. The nearest oasis or water supply that he knew, apart from that seeping spring back on the horizon, was at Bir Khula, where his friends were. That was two days' ride south, through hostile, Arab country.

Riding up to that nearby oasis that he was watching was out of the question, of course. Last night he had seen Captain Sturmer there, vicious, bloody-minded

Sturmer, the Nazi, with his renegade Arab *partizans* who were employed as bloodhounds to track down deserters.

Nope, he decided, he wasn't going into that oasis, not in broad daylight. He considered the possibilities of a night attack, a foray to get food and drink and perhaps capture Sturmer. A hazardous adventure, with the almost certain fate of detection, capture and death to follow. He'd decided to risk it, because more than anything else, he was determined to get Sturmer before a war criminals' court, when suddenly Mahfra gripped his arm urgently.

Her big, soft brown eyes were bigger than usual. There was shock in them.

Tex squinted against the sun once again, for she was looking south-east of their position, and that was the direction of the climbing sun at the moment. He saw dust figures . . . mounted men . . .

'Arabs!'

Thousands of them, probably Nuhas Pasha's entire army. White-robed, burnoused men, milling into position behind a ridge of sand.

Tex looked to the oasis. There'd be sentries, of course, but he couldn't see any. He saw lots of men strolling above and relaxing after their long march through the night. Nuhas Pasha was going to catch that small force napping.

The American looked again at those Arabs. They were forming into battle line, out of sight of the Legion troops

Tex thought, 'The hell, this ain't my war!' He didn't kid himself that because he had joined the Legion and was technically still of it, he owed allegiance to France. The way he'd been treated, though no differently from any other Legionnaire, of course, didn't leave him with any feelings of sympathy for France's position as colonial administrator. His sympathies were with the Arabs — again not necessarily with the Arab leaders, who struck him as great a poison to their own kin as the French, but with the ordinary people who lived out such dreary, uncomfortable lives.

Yet now he found he couldn't sit there and watch unwary men be shot down before they had chance to get into position where they could defend themselves. He felt there was an absence of logic about the way his thoughts ran but at times instinct was stronger than reason. Now was one of those times.

He called down to Louie, 'There's an army of Ay-rabs about to beat the daylights outa the Legion in that oasis. I figger on gettin' a warnin' out to 'em. I'm gonna fire a shot!'

Tex retired to the back of the cave, taking the girl with him. He didn't want smoke to betray his position. He lifted the Lebel that he had brought up with him sighted at the patch of brilliant blue sky, and fired.

Dust danced, the echoes reverberated for a few seconds but the smoke hung back and didn't stir towards the cave mouth. Satisfied, the acrid bite of cordite in his nostrils, Tex crept to the mouth of the cave and peered out. What he saw satisfied him.

His warning shot had alerted the French troops. Men were rushing about in a manner that Tex knew too well. He even heard the whistles as sergeants went calling men to action stations, and then a bugler added to the sound. At least these Legionnaires wouldn't be caught napping; they'd have a chance of saving their lives.

Tex looked south-east, to where the Arabs were. Either they hadn't heard the shot, because of their own many sounds, or else it was ignored. They were still getting into line — or rather, into two lines.

About ten minutes later, two things happened. First, the Arabs, on a signal, rode to the crest of that ridge. Immediately, as if they had only been waiting for that confirmation of the threat of attack, a cavalcade of horsemen spurred out northwards from the oasis, into the hot, yellow desert.

They were Arabs, all but their leader, who wore Arab headdress but a legion-blue uniform. In all there were about thirty of them, and Tex knew them at a glance.

This would be Captain Sturmer, riding out with his renegade *partizans*. Of course it was well known in the Legion that the *partizans* avoided all battle with their own kind. They weren't to be trusted, anyway, but also their duties were to track down deserters and also to act as an intelligence unit in the desert.

Automatically, at this prospect of attack, Sturmer had ridden out with his forces. Tex watched him strike north, and he was in agony. Here was his enemy riding away from him, and he couldn't do anything to stop him. And going north was no good to him — that way were only more and more Legion armies, and he was an ex-Legionnaire, with a price upon his head as a deserter.

His attention swung back from those retreating *partizans*. Those thousands of Arab horsemen, silhouetted against the blue Sahara sky on that long, wind-scoured ridge of yellow sand, had begun their charge.

Fascinated, with a grandstand view of the battle up there on the rock, they saw the rolling clouds of dust, the flutter of many-coloured Arab robes, the multi-coloured effect of black, grey, white, brown and piebald horses. It was a moving patchwork of colour.

They heard, suddenly, the mighty roar of the charging desert warriors — 'Allah above all! Death to the infidel!'

Within that oasis there was no movement now. Thanks to that warning shot the Legionnaires were in position to defend themselves. Fascinated, Tex saw puffs of smoke, then a rapid rattle of gunfire. Machine guns. He saw gaps grow in the ranks of those Arabs, saw men and horses go down.

He felt a horror inside him, because he felt responsible for this. He had warned his former comrades of the Legion and saved their lives, but at the expense of Arabs. And he bore no ill will towards these desert people, had only sympathy with them for the hard life they had to lead.

He took off his kepi and wiped the sweat from the band. It was a terrifying spectacle, to see men in a win-or-die battle; fascinating, so that he couldn't take his eyes off the scene. And yet he hated it. He'd seen enough of war in this desert, and wanted no more of it.

The second wave of Arabs was racing forward now, guns blazing, charging recklessly, courageously towards that dark green oasis. Again those machine guns chattered death, and holes were blasted in the ranks of the attackers. This time they weren't driven away, however; this time a wave of men swept in under the palm trees with their listless, drooping, dusty leaves. With fanatical courage they raced in and attacked the Legionnaires at close quarters.

It was too far to see the details, but Tex could imagine what was happening. Now that most savage and terrible of war weapons, the bayonet, would be in play. Desperate, harassed Legionnaires would be back to back, thrusting, lunging, parrying, swinging with the butts of their heavy Lebels. Screaming, wild-eyed, bearded Arabs would be stooping from their saddles, their terrible swords swinging and hacking, blue-tunicked men falling beneath the sharp hooves of their horses.

Men would be falling and dying and shouting out their last agonies, asking heaven why they had ever got themselves into such stupidity . . . would be asking it in many languages, and thinking of many different heavens.

Horses would be hamstrung, would be falling crippled and dying, and screaming their pain and terror — and perhaps thinking in their way, 'What have we done to be treated so?'

That was war. Tex had seen it in North Africa, in Sicily and Italy and right through France into Germany. Anybody could have war for him. Just bring the war criminals to justice, that was all he could think of right then, watching that battle. It was the leaders on both sides who were no good to anybody except themselves, certainly no good for the people whose destinies they were supposed to control and safeguard. The curse of men was they couldn't rest until they had power . . .

Horrified, Tex's mental soliloquy came to an end. For Legion Captain Herman Sturmer was staring up at him.

6

Watching that battle, Tex and the girl hadn't seen the manoeuvre of the *partizan* leader and his men. They had come circling from the north, and were now trotting along the foot of the big rock outcrop. They were out of sight of the battle, and heading southwards.

Tex wasn't to know what was in the captain's mind but Sturmer's thoughts were exclusively for him and a newspaperwoman who had pictures, which in the end could effect his extradition from the Legion.

That girl was Monica Shaw — Nicky to Tex and his deserter comrades, now at the Oasis Bir Khula.

Nicky had taken dozens of pictures of Sturmer. If they ever got back to America and were published, American opinion would force the French authorities to hand the Legion officer over to international justice. They wouldn't like doing that — it was said that the French never handed back a criminal once he had joined the Legion. But Herman Sturmer knew he was an exceptional criminal, knew that America was a powerful country since the end of the war and guessed that France, who didn't love Nazi generals anyway, would in the end capitulate and give Sturmer over to the hangman.

Sturmer, who had taken many lives, had a rooted objection to losing his. So he was now moving south as rapidly as he could. He wanted to get those pictures from Nicky Shaw — and silence all those who knew his identity.

A bold man, though he looked more like a peevish thin-faced clerk than a resourceful and ferocious general Sturmer saw in this battle in the desert the opportunity he needed. He would circle round the mighty Arab army while it was engaged in fighting; to the south there would be few Arab warriors now, he guessed, so that he would be able to travel to Bir Khula without molestation.

He didn't know the deserters and the

newspaper girl were at the oasis, but he'd heard mention of a waterhole when he was being taken south a prisoner, only a few days before and Bir Khula was the only one he knew in that direction. He thought that if he reached the oasis, he would be able pick up the trail there.

With his freshly-recruited force of *partizans*, he was riding rapidly round the Arab flank, at any moment now turning south to Bir Khula.

He was leading his men along the foot of the big sandstone cliff, when his sharp eye detected a movement and looked up. He saw the dark openings where the cave dwellers used to live, and then saw two heads. As he looked, a face turned down towards him, looking straight in his direction

Tex dropped flat, immediately. Horrified, he saw Mahfra do the wrong thing. Impulsively, acting on curiosity, she stretched outwards, to see what had made Tex behave so

She was fully exposed from her waist upwards to the view of the *partizans* and their chief below. Tex grabbed her, pulled her down beside him, but he knew it was too late. Anyway, Sturmer must have seen him, Tex, before that indiscretion of Mahfra's. His hand reached for his Lebel, and knocked the safety catch off. He waited for the sharp word of command that would tell of fierce *partizans* being sent to scale the cliff and rout him out.

None came.

Sturmer had seen those two faces. One had looked pink and un-Arab like. That one had ducked out of sight, but he'd seen it. The other had stretched upwards, suddenly, and he was able to see that she was unmistakably an Arab woman.

He shrugged. A couple of cave dwellers, was how he dismissed them. He went riding on, turning now southward. In two days he would be at Bir Khula. If necessary he'd follow the deserters and that interfering newspaper girl all the way to Lake Chad, which was supposed to be the route of this suicidal party.

He thought of them, cynically. All Americans. A flat-faced man with a yapping voice from Brooklyn — an ex-boxer probably. Rube, a man known as The Schemer, because he was forever, as these Americans said, cooking up bright ideas. And Dimmy, a slow-witted, good-natured man who had been shot and hurt very badly. Perhaps he was dead now.

Sturmer hoped not. He merely hoped he was very severely wounded. He didn't hope this for any charitable reasons but from a tactical point of view.

You travelled slowly with a wounded man.

High above them, two pairs of eyes, one pair narrowed and grey, the other big round and warmly brown, followed the *partizans* to the horizon.

Then they came down that gully at a breakneck pace. They found a white-faced, agonized Louie below, waiting for them.

Louie exclaimed, 'Oh, god, Tex, did you see what I saw? Sturmer?' Tex nodded, going for their horses. Louie almost whispered, 'I was within ten yards of him. I thought he'd seen me, thought for certain he was gonna come in here, then my number'd have been up.'

Tex helped him into the saddle. He was still trembling from the shock. Almost better than any other man, Louie of the camel face knew what little mercy lay in the heart of that ex-Nazi. If Louie had been detected, literally he would have lost his head within five seconds.

Just a snap of those thin fingers. There'd have been a mad scramble on the part of his bloodthirsty warriors, their dreaded *flissas* flashing. It would have been like throwing meat to a pack of starving wolves only he, Louie, would have been the meat — and his head would have been the prize they sought.

He kept rubbing his neck as they cantered out on to the desert, as if not sure it was still safe. He was in a bitter mood, a very ill man since his torture by those women.

Tex knew the man should have been put into a hospital bed and rested, but he couldn't see many hospitals and this was no place for rest, so he had to keep him riding.

That white face with its long yellow teeth came round anxiously and Louie

120

asked, 'We're going after Sturmer, Tex — why?'

Tex answered with a shrug, 'It's as good a place as any to go — an' I want Sturmer.'

Louie whimpered a bit from fear, but there wasn't anything he could do about it. They set off in the trampled hoofmarks of the *partizans*. Because of Louie's condition, Tex had to go at a steady pace, and he knew there was little chance of catching up with his enemy. All the same, he breasted each rise cautiously, and surveyed the country beyond before proceeding.

Mahfra never said a word, but went to sleep. She'd seen the desert all her life, and didn't see any sense in looking at it when she could be sleeping. So long as she was with this mighty Americano, who treated her with kindness, she didn't care where they went.

Before she fell asleep she thought of the stories that had drifted into her village, of the fabulously wealthy Americanos, all of whom had several automobiles, palaces for houses, as much water as they wanted to drink, and so much grass they could keep cattle by the million. And none ever took more than one wife.

Now, that was heaven to Mahfra, and she sighed in ecstasy at the thought. She fell asleep praying that the Americano who had taken her to be his would be just such a wealthy Americano.

Tex would have had a shock if he had known the thoughts that were going on in her young and pretty head.

They slept during the hours of darkness, but rose and proceeded on their way when the moon was up. It was eerie work, riding on the bare white slopes or through the long, velvety black shadows, but it was preferable to traveling the whole day long under the broiling sun. Tex guessed that the *partizans* were also travelling by night, and again did not fear that they would run into the headhunters. Louie feared all the time.

Louie was ill and in terror, but there was nothing Tex could do to help him. One of Louie's fears was about the reception he'd get when they joined up with his former comrades in the oasis at Bir Khula.

He kept saying, contritely, 'I was a heel. I did a terrible thing, Tex, walkin' out on you like I did an' helpin' them *partizans*. But I was scared — scared to hell. I didn't know what I was doin'.'

Over and over the same ground, all the time. Tex got sick of it, wearied of the man's self-abasement, but tried not to show it.

All he could say, to this man who had nearly cost him and his comrades their lives, was, 'Quit worryin', fellar. Maybe they'll gripe a bit, but they won't hurt you.'

Gripe? When pug-faced Joe Ellighan from Brooklyn saw him, he'd give Louie the Camel a mouthful, all right!

Louie fell asleep in his saddle after that, hanging on somehow, but rolling from side to side. The girl slept most of the time, too, nestling against Tex. She was like a kitten, curling up and sleeping at will, Tex thought. He looked at her face in the moonlight as she slept. She was pretty enough for anything; back in the States she sure would have the wolves whistling.

It made him muse philosophically for a while, that this lovely creature, because by accident of birth she should be born in the middle of this desert that was as big as the United States itself, should be denied the pleasures and freedom of her Western sisters. Mahfra might never in her life know the feel of nylons on her slim and shapely legs, never see a movie or ride in an automobile . . . she'd live a hard life, marrying and having children the hard way, never having a holiday, becoming prematurely old because of the sun that burnt the life out of them . . .

Startled, he realized that he had been dropping to sleep himself. It was so easy, sitting there, with the horses plodding patiently along, in a rhythm that in time became hypnotic.

He jerked back his head. Mahfra was slipping from his grasp. She began to stir, to waken. He looked ahead. Mahfra opened her lovely brown eyes, saw that lean face under the kepi in the moonlight, and smiled adoringly at him.

Her soft red lips opened, her teeth

sparkled in the cold white light. She began to say, 'Takes . . . '

And then the American put his hand across her mouth, and his strong left arm gripped her and kept her still. Fear came into those lovely eyes, then . . .

Tex looked down at her. She saw his grey eyes, then his head was nodding significantly ahead. He had reined in his horse; Louie's had halted without any further ado. Louie sat lolling in the saddle, fast asleep.

The girl looked across a sea of shadows and rounded white hills. Along a ridge a quarter of a mile ahead of them a party of Arabs was riding. They were strung out, heading southwards, the way Tex and his companions were travelling

The girl stopped struggling, and Tex removed his hand He was counting those silent, shrouded horsemen — one, two three . . . four, five, six. Could be, he was thinking, these 'Ay-rabs' were Ca-ca and his renegade followers. The Legionnaires had disturbed them and driven them out from that oasis back of them, and now they would be roaming the desert in search of some other resting place.

There weren't many resting places in the Sahara. He didn't envy the renegades. They were heading south. He thought, 'Maybe they're trustin' to luck an' goin' to throw themselves on the mercy of their Arab friends.'

It was a dangerous thing to do, but the renegades would have to do something if they were to survive — must find some place with water for themselves and beasts, and food too.

Tex thought, 'Bir Khula's ahead.'

This was becoming complicated. If these six silent horsemen were the renegades, and they were heading for the Oasis Bir Khula, they would find his comrades, Rube, Dimmy and Elegant there, along with the newspaperwoman. That would spell trouble.

Watching those horsemen dissolve into the darkness he realized suddenly that Captain Sturmer and his ferocious cutthroats were also heading roughly in the direction of Bir Khula. The thought came to him, 'We don't need to trail Sturmer any more!' It seemed pretty certain that the *partizans* were headed for Bir Khula oasis, and now Tex knew why.

Sturmer was going after the deserters, his comrades probably thinking that he, Tex, was still with them.

Tex woke Louie at that. He shook him and spoke urgently. 'Louie, we've got to make better speed. We've got to get ahead of Sturmer, somehow, an' warn Rube an' the boys that Sturmer's after their heads. Can you hang on if we go faster?'

Louie nodded dully. Tex got the horses into better speed, heading eastwards gradually, so that they were away from the tracks of both Sturmer's *partizans* and the supposed Legion renegades. Tex merely hoped the two forces would run into each other. That would settle a lot of problems, but didn't think there'd be any such luck.

They rode all night, and then continued while ever they could the next day after the sun rose. Mahfra grew petulant the long hours in the saddle, but Tex ignored her. It was now a race to warn his friends of the double danger that was closing on them.

They made such good pace that day,

that by noon of the following day they were within sight of the palm tops that announced the oasis in the desert. Tex went even farther east then, so as to come upon Bir Khula from a point distant from the main village within it. He had been to Bir Khula before on Legion patrol, and remembered it well.

They rode openly up to the oasis, simply because there was nothing else for it. Perhaps because of the very openness of the approach, they got away with it. No bunch of hard-riding Arabs came out to take a shot at those hated blue uniforms. Probably, Tex reasoned, most males were away with the army, anyway, and so that reduced the number of possible eyes to watch the desert.

They rode gratefully in under the shade of those thickly clustered palm trees. Bir Khula was an oasis of considerable importance. A small river gushed out of a mountainside, and ran a couple of miles before disappearing once again into the desert. Intensive irrigation had given a cultivated area that was two miles long and in parts over a mile wide. Several thousand people living within the shade of the tall palm trees, most in a sprawling village situated to the west of the oasis.

When they were in among the inevitable thorn scrub, which precluded the irrigated, cultivated area, they dismounted wearily. They were caked in sweat and dust, and they had been so long in the saddle that their limbs creaked as they moved them.

For a time they just lay wearily in the shade and shelter of some tall spear-leafed bushes, while Tex planned their next move.

It wouldn't do for them to walk openly through to the village, because with this war flaring up between Arab and the French there might be unpleasant reactions from the local populace. Tex didn't want to be knifed or shot before he had a chance to open his mouth. Though he wondered what he would say if he did open his mouth.

So he sent Mahfra on a scouting expedition. After all, she was going to come in useful. First, though, she went to the dying stream that was draining away about this point in the loose sandy soil of the thirsty desert. She filled the skin water-containers and returned with them. Then she set off to learn what she could about Tex's friends.

Tex and Louie drank gratefully, drinking all that their parched frames could take. Then they squirted water into the mouths of their horses, trained to accept it this way and standing eagerly with mouths agape to take the life-giving stream.

After that, horse and man felt better, and the horses began to crop at any vegetation that was eatable, while the two men lay down and rested.

They came hurriedly to their feet when Mahfra padded quickly back to them with her report. She sat down tired from her long walk through the oasis and back. She pushed back her luxuriant black hair from her brown, handsome face, and then told them the news.

Tex's friends were in prison.

7

Mahfra had intelligence. She'd guessed that Tex's first reaction would be to go and speak to his friends, so she had brought an Arab burnouse with her as a disguise. She objected a bit when he announced that he would go alone, though. She looked at Louie with apprehension and whispered that she liked him not. But Tex wasn't going to be cluttered up with females on this trip, and he told her so and she had to accept his decision.

He left the Lebel with Louie, gave money to Mahfra and left her with instructions to forage around and buy food for a possible long journey.

He went afoot, too. He had a feeling that a horse would be an encumbrance on a scouting expedition around the prison, though he didn't relish the long walk.

Covering his uniform with that all-enveloping Arab cloak, and hiding his face behind a white mouth-cloth that went with the burnouse, he set off through the palm trees. After a while he came to a path that led alongside the cultivated fields — a patchwork of small, intensively cultivated plots, each bordered by a water channel, that led to a main irrigation stream, which in turn obtained water from the sparkling, swift-running little river.

There were men working in the fields, bare-legged because of the need to stand in much water, and women, too, with their black dresses hitched up so that they could stoop and perform their back-breaking work. They didn't look up at the solitary 'Arab' who stalked silently by. Tex, waiting for reaction, was relieved to find that his presence didn't excite comment when he passed another traveller along the pathway — an old man with a donkey, burdened with soil that was being moved to a more advantageous site.

Then he met more and more people — men, women and children — as he got nearer the village, and these, too, ignored him. His disguise was sufficient. He exulted. He would be able to speak with his friends at will, from what Mahfra had told him, and get away safely afterwards.

Soon he came into the Arab village. There were tented dwellings on the outside, and then came the usual flat-topped, mud-walled buildings that were drab and ugly individually and yet gave the village a curious charm. Tex thought, perhaps it was this sunlight, bright but not too strong upon them, because of the dappling shadows of the surrounding tall palms.

But he didn't dwell long upon the subtle beauties of that village amid the luxuriant greenery. He had a job to do, and he went resolutely about it.

He forded the river that ran through the village. It was full of naked brown children splashing and swimming and enjoying life. It wasn't quite credible that these children would become the ferocious warriors of the desert that their fathers were.

Women were knee deep in the water, washing garments and sometimes babies or themselves. Tex heard their voices, chattering unceasingly among themselves. Women at work were all the same.

He noticed there weren't many men about. Most of the warriors would be away north, with Nuhas Pasha. He wondered how they had fared in the battle with the Legion in that other oasis whose name he didn't know.

Right through the village he strode, following the directions that Mahfra had given him, passing the few shops where traders sat cross-legged before their pitiful array of goods, past the long, chewing lines of camels waiting to be loaded with produce for distant markets, past farriers and metal workers toiling at their forges. He felt he would have liked time to wander round this Arab village. It was interesting, unspoiled, not at all like the *villages negres* that were around the Legion posts.

He found the place where his friends were incarcerated without difficulty. It was one of the sheik's houses, though he was not to know that until later.

It was a house set aside to receive these

unusual prisoners, a rather more solid-looking dwelling than the others, isolated a little from other buildings, with long glassless windows that were heavily barred, and with guards at the doors, front and rear.

The guards didn't make much of their job, however. There were three of them at the front, and one at the back. Tex walked round the building from a distance, making his manner as casual as possible, stopping sometimes to look at the wares offered for sale by fly-pestered Arab traders.

The three guards in front were playing a game with small stones on a pattern traced out in the sandy soil. They were squatting together, at ease, their rifles propped against the big, barred door behind them.

The guard at the rear was unashamedly asleep. Evidently these guards thought little of their job.

Tex realized that if he went to one side of the house he would be out of view of both guards. A barred window there would permit him to talk with the occupants. Slowly he began to move away from the stalls, his grey eyes watching all around him for possible danger.

Yet missing it — bringing danger to him because few Arabs have grey eyes.

A bearded, hungry-looking Arab who was trained not to miss a thing, turned and followed him and watched him from a distance.

Tex strolled casually up to that window. He glanced round. He was almost out of sight of everyone. Risking a lot, he stood against that barred window and looked in.

He saw a bare room, with a few mats on the floor and no other furnishings. Two men were lying on their stomachs, playing cards and arguing noisily. Both wore the white pantaloons of the Legion, but nothing else.

Tex saw a battered mug yapping as the owner slapped down a decisive card. That was Joe — Legionnaire Ellighan, sometimes known as Elegant. The figure with his back to him would be Rube, The Schemer.

He was disappointed. Neither Dimmy

nor the girl was there. He badly wanted to see that girl again, see her fresh, golden beauty, her clear, flawless complexion and cool, Nordic eyes.

But she wasn't there. His heart chilled a little. She would be especially desirable to the menfolk of this dark-skinned, black-haired people.

He adjusted his thoughts. Looked down into the cool room and drawled, 'I figger they've got a bridge in Sydney, Australia, that sure licks any other bridge in the world.'

Elegant got excited. He slapped down his cards and yapped, 'That don't resemble the truth. It's a goddam lie. The finest bridge in all the woild is the Brooklyn bridge . . . '

He stopped. Something was dawning on him. It had already dawned upon the quick-witted Rube, that fresh-faced, blue-eyed young American of Polish ancestry, who was known as The Schemer.

Rube was up at the window like a shot, his eyes beaming, his hands reaching out to grasp his comrade's.

'Tex, you old longhorn maverick!' he

exclaimed. 'It's good to see you again. Gosh, have we been waitin' for this moment!'

His eyes took in the disguise, and his face fell, disappointed. 'Looks like you ain't on friendly terms with these Arabs, either,' he ended.

Tex looked round. There was just one Arab strolling in the distance. He risked more time at the window. Spoke urgently.

'I've got two hosses back there along the oasis; there'll be chow an' water for us all if you c'n get outa here.' He didn't tell about Louie and the Arab girl. There'd be time enough for that later.

'You didn't get Sturmer?' Tex had left his comrades to go on the trail of his enemy.

'Sturmer's somewhere aroun'. Mebbe he's in this oasis like we are.' Tex looked again over his shoulder. Just that one Arab preparing to lie down and sleep in the shade in the distance. 'An' Ca-Ca an' his mob are somewhere in the vicinity.'

Elegant's flat face was up at the bars now. He said, in that thin colourless yap that passed for a voice, 'Then we got nice company around, Tex!'

The ex-cowboy now asked the question uppermost in his mind. 'How's Dimmy, an' where's Nicky?'

For answer Elegant went and fetched both. Apparently the prisoners could go at will throughout the house, and Nicky was bandaging Dimmy Dimicci's wounds at that moment.

While Elegant was gone, Rube told his story. 'This war breakin' out kinda queered plans,' An Arab, son of the sheik of Bir Khula, in gratefulness for being rescued by Tex, had promised to lead the ex-Legionnaires to the coast and give them safe conduct through Arab territory. That had been the plan. But Rube explained . . .

'You know how it is, Tex, when a people go to war. They kinda forget to be so friendly, I reckon. When we came ridin' in with 'brahim, the people wanted to take a poke at us, but I reckon 'brahim's old man is pretty powerful an' when he said no, we were not to be touched because his son had given his word we were not to be harmed, the crowd let us alone.

'He's a pretty fine old boy, 'brahim's poppa. White-bearded an' intelligent. I gather he's agen this war, says Right is with the Arab people but the French have got too many machine guns an' other weapons. He slapped us in jail more to protect us than to keep us here.

'You see, Tex, we said we wouldn't go on without you, an' the sheik figgered if we got to strollin' aroun' the oasis we'd sure run into trouble from some of the hotheads.'

Tex nodded. His eyes were watching that doorway across from the window. 'Does that mean you c'n go any time you like?'

''brahim says it'd be tactful if we kinda bust outa jail; says it would save his father the embarrassment of releasing us. Elegant figgers he c'n bust out if he c'n get some ammunition. That's all he needs to make a nice li'l bomb that'll blow a man-sized hole in the back wall.'

Elegant had his ammunition from that moment. Tex passed it through the window, all the spare revolver ammunition he owned on him. It left him short,

140

but there was no alternative. He would have to replace it when he could.

The door opened. Nicky Shaw came in. Back of her, grinning amiably, was Dimmy Dimicci, his head bandaged, another bandage showing under his open shirt.

Nicky ran forward. She was in light grey slacks, wearing a fresh-laundered white blouse. She looked cool and fresh and lovely. Tex saw sparkling eyes that were as blue as the Mediterranean, saw her pink and white complexion that was in such contrast to these Semites' around him.

Then she grasped his hand through the bars, saying, fervently, 'It's good to see you again, Tex.'

He said, softly, 'Nicky, it's good to see you, too!'

She said, 'We've only been waiting for you to catch up with us before we broke out of jail — or tried to . . . '

This was no time for speeches. At any moment someone might come round the corner and discover him speaking with the prisoners. Even with that lax guard, it

141

wasn't a risk to run if avoidable.

Tex said, 'I'm goin'. I'll get hosses for you all. They'll be back of the jail exactly the moment the moon rises. Blow a hole in the wall, then, Elly, an' come out runnin'!'

Elly nodded. Tex was worrying about weapons. They'd have none, and the desert was no place for the party without guns. Not with Sturmer and his head-hunters on the prowl after their scalps, and Ca-ca and his evil-hearted renegades to roam the desert because the way to the coast was now blocked for them by two armies.

But there was nothing he could do about that. He started away hurriedly. He didn't want to be detected now. It was vital to their plans that he secured horses for the party. As he left them, he heard Nicky's voice . . . ''brahim wants to come with us, Tex.' 'brahim, the Arab, son of the sheik, who had befriended them. He'd fallen for the American girl heavily, which was to be expected. Now it seemed he wanted to leave the country with them. Tex put that little matter in a corner of his mind, for him to think about later.

Tex gathered his robe carefully around him, and strode off through the winding village. He walked carefully, so that his heavy Legion boots did not show when he strode out, and the white mouth-cloth that was used to keep the desert sands out of the lungs of the wearer effectually screened most of his face.

Now he didn't fear detection.

He was in the centre of the village, a couple of hundred yards from the prison house, at a place where the street ran alongside the cool, pleasant river. Here were cafés where lordly males sat over their coffee or sucked on the bubble pipes or played backgammon. There were many people about, for time for siesta was past and the village was waking up.

Tex heard a patter of sandalled feet behind him, as someone hurried up to him. He didn't turn. He didn't think it concerned him. A brown, sinewy hand reached out and took hold of his Arab robe and pulled. It was dragged open.

Right before that crowd of café patrons

he was revealed as a man wearing white drill trousers, blue tunic and military belt . . . was revealed as a Legionnaire, the traditional Arab enemy.

Tables crashed, chairs went over, a raw-throated shout of hatred went up from those fierce-eyed men. Hands dived under flowing robes and came out with flashing knives and swords.

Tex wheeled, his muscles bunching. He saw a man falling away from him, a man who was satisfied that he had done his work and there was no further need for him to stay.

An Arab — a turbanned Arab with the dust still on him that came from a long ride across desert sands. A long-faced man with sharp brown eyes and a fringe of beard that ran from ear to ear and yet was no more than an inch long even on his chin. Tex saw that face and the cruelty in the soul of that man through it.

His immediate thoughts were, 'This guy looks mean enough to be a *partizan*. He's got the cutthroat look.' And at once he knew he was right.

This was a *partizan*. Sturmer and his

144

force must already be in hiding nearby . . . This man would be a scout, and he had betrayed the secret of his disguise.

Tex jumped straight for the *partizan*. He moved quickly, too quickly for the man. The *partizan's* mouth opened in alarm and he went for a dagger. Tex's big boot caught him as he was trying to turn and flee. The man yelped in alarm, lost his balance, and went into the water. There was quite a touch of comedy in the scene.

Tex didn't wait for the laughs, however. He turned and hurtled back the way he had come. The uproar behind grew to a tremendous volume. Women added to it with screams, though they couldn't have known what they were screaming about. Children shrieked and had a fine old time.

Tex saw the way ahead barred by a suddenly looming barrier of people. He ran into a house, through the wide hall that ran through it, and came out on a back street beyond

He was at the end of it when he saw a crowd of Arabs spring from nowhere to block his path. He jumped a fence, crossed a narrow patch that was soggy to his heavy boots — and more Arabs came running towards him.

He was surrounded, in the middle of the village, and there was no escape. He turned the only way open to him, and found himself in a familiar place. Right in front was the jail wherein were his comrades. He saw anxious faces pressing to the barred windows. Elegant's. Rube's. Dimmy's bandaged head. And the golden head of Nicky Shaw.

Because there was no other way of escape, he walked forward to the big, closed door of that prison house, walked past the guards who looked up from their game and stared at him and then at the big crowd pressing up behind him. When he reached the door he stood with his back to it and drew out his revolver.

It was useless, of course, as a weapon. If he wished he could kill a few people and hurt others, but that wouldn't stop this mob from tearing him to pieces afterwards. He used it as a threat, though, to keep that ravening mob away from his throat. He'd never hankered after being torn in bits by any crazy lot of sadists.

The crowd stayed back twenty yards from that threatening blue muzzle. They set up a constant uproar, each urging the other to be first to strike down this spy in their midst, this hated Legionnaire. But for a few minutes no one moved to attack, no one relished the role of martyr, and that gun looked capable of making the first half-dozen to jump forward figure in the central position at a funeral.

Above the raging fury of the crowd, Tex began to hear a voice shouting behind him. Nicky was at the door. But he couldn't tell what she was saying . . . she couldn't do anything to help him, anyway.

Back of the crowd he saw a familiar face, that *partizan* with the inch-long beard that looked like a ruff round his cheeks. There were others with the man now, others who had the same stamp. Half a dozen of them.

Tex bellowed, 'The hell, see what you get for startin' all this!'

He had no compunction so far as the *partizans* were concerned; he was in a tight spot, with his life probably forfeit in a moment, anyway. He let rip with his revolver, three quick rounds that sent the crowd scampering, and the *partizans* diving for the cover of a building.

Now in the comparative silence while people acted and hadn't time for their tongue, he heard Nicky's voice. 'You shouldn't have done that, Tex. Get 'brahim to shove you inside with us. We can escape later.'

Without someone on the outside to get horses and have them ready? All the same, he was glad he had shoved that ammunition through the bars. If he could get stuck away, that gave them a chance of bursting out when they chose.

Suddenly 'brahim was there before him. Tex saw that dark bearded face under the white burnouse and his face lit up. 'brahim was a man of courage, for all he was young. In front of that hostile crowd, he had guts enough to come forward, smiling, his hand outstretched in welcome.

Tex holstered his gun, grinned and took that hand. He said dryly, 'Brother, you've got a nerve. This'll put you on a limb, I reckon.'

'brahim must have understood, though he spoke little English. He said, simply, 'Tek-suss saved my life on more than one occasion. He will be my friend forever. I have no shame at showing it before my people.'

His people were crowding nearer now. encouraged by the absence of that weapon. Tex's eyes watched them while he spoke with the young man.

'I cannot escape.'

'brahim shrugged. 'I would not attempt it. Give me your gun.'

Tex hated to part with this weapon, but he knew that his Arab friend was right. He trusted him, too. 'brahim wouldn't play dirty on him: like, for instance, his own countryman, Louie, had done.

He withdrew the gun again and handed it to the sheik's son. At once the crowd came flooding forward. 'brahim wheeled and faced them, flinging up his hands for silence. He knew how to command. They halted again, a sullen, suspicious-eyed mob.

Tex caught the drift of that clear-spoken Arabic. 'This man is my friend. I know he is a cursed infidel, that he was until recently in the ranks of the hated French. But he is not at heart with our oppressors. He has left them and will not again fight for them. He is an American, and wishes to return to his own country.

'This Americano saved my life, not once but continuously, when I was hiding from the Legion. For that I must give my life if necessary to save his.' That little gun came up in his hands at that, and he said, 'If necessary, I will.'

That kept the crowd where they were. This young Arab was courageous, resourceful, a man of honour. He would keep his word and would die in an attempt to keep his friend from harm, they knew.

But they grew angry with him. There were those who said such friendships were wrong and traitorous. They said no matter what the cunning infidel had done, 'brahim should not stand in their way now. For weren't they at death-grips again with the foreigner, and was there time now for such sentiments?

150

'Kill!' they shouted, mob-like. 'Death to the infidel!'

But that didn't move the young Arab. He stood and waited for the first man to come forward to lay a hand on his friend, the Americano.

All the same — and Tex was quick to recognize it — in time that mob would have come driving forward, impelled by those safely to the rear. They would overrun 'brahim and put their clawing, murderous hands upon their victim.

At which moment the sheik of Bir Khula came out from the crowd. Tex guessed him to be the sheik at once. He saw a dignified, white-bearded old Arab who held his robes about him like a king. Tex's eyes lifted to the *agal*, that headrope that held in position the Arab headdress, the kafir.

This was no ordinary thing of horse-hair, but a white rope of silk bound together by golden threads. The mark of the sheik.

'brahim salaamed respectfully. The sheik spoke, quickly — too quickly for Tex to follow. 'brahim went forward a few

151

paces and conversed with his father. In a moment the sheik had made his decision.

He, too, was not afraid to take action that made him unpopular. He clapped his hands, and the guard came running over from where they had been standing back with the crowd.

'brahim came back to Tex, grinning. 'You are to be put into jail on my father's orders,' he explained. 'It is for your own safety. My father has agreed that tomorrow there should be a meeting of the elders of the tribe to discuss your fate.'

His brown eyes twinkled in that black-bearded face.

'Perhaps it would be as well if the prisoners escaped during the night, for with this war to inflame even our elders' minds, they might come to a decision I would regret and could not accept.'

Tex murmured, 'I would regret it too, brother.' The guards were unlocking that big, paintless door.

'brahim spoke again. There was anxiety in his voice. 'Will you, do you think, be able to get out of this prison?'

'We can escape whenever we want,' said Tex confidently.

'Then I will have horses ready for you when you need them.'

'We'll be needin' 'em the moment the moon comes up in the east. Keep 'em in the bushes at the back of the jail. And, brother, you're a pal; I never expect to meet a better!'

'brahim just said, earnestly, 'My debt is nowhere near repaid. I will go with you at least to the border, perhaps right to the coast.'

Then he left before Tex had time to get his thoughts round to Mahfra and the camel-faced Legionnaire at the east end of the oasis.

The door swung open, and the guards stood on one side. Tex saw Nicky standing in the middle of that doorway. She looked so fair and lovely, blonde, fresh-complexioned, and clean-looking in her grey slacks and white blouse, and there was an instant gasp of admiration from the Arab males in the forefront of the crowd.

She started to run out, Rube, Elly and

the bandaged Dimmy pressing on her heels, but the guards swung old muzzle-loaders at them, and they stayed on the threshold. Tex just shrugged and walked into the prison. The door slammed on them. He hoped his prophecy would be good, hoped they could get out as easily as he had said.

For he felt certain that any trial before the elders of the tribe would have only one result, with their minds inflamed by this war to the north.

Death for the infidels!

Death for the Legionnaires, but perhaps another fate for the American girl.

Inside they crowded round him, slapping his back and congratulating him on his escape from the mob. He told what had happened, removing the Arab burnouse that was too warm over the top of his uniform.

He sat down against a wall that was in the shadow. The others grouped round him, Nicky at his feet, the others sprawled on the mats alongside. Now they had leisure they could go into details.

There wasn't much more for them to

tell him about their incarceration here in the prison house. The Arabs, because of the sheik's orders, had been kind to them, but daily the temper of the inhabitants had grown worse. They had heard people shouting against them, the previous night, from a meeting not over far from the prison house. There were people who were trying to stir the mob up to seize and kill them.

Then it was Tex's turn to tell his story.

When he got as far as his meeting Mahfra, there were long whistles and wolf calls from the boys.

'You say she's a peach?' — Rube, interested.

'She's a wow,' said Tex. 'You wait till you see her.'

Nicky said, 'I don't like this a bit. The heck, I came to the Sahara to get rid of competition.' Then she fluffed out her hair, provocatively. ''brahim says he'll make me marry him. He swears he's going back to cut his beard off and come back to America with us and marry me.'

'Yeah?' Tex looked at that pretty face. There was a twinkle in his own eyes.

'What am I gonna do to let him?'

'You?' It was Rube. 'Brother, you lost your chances when you walked out on us. Me, I've been putting in some nice work all that time since.'

Elegant's pan shone with enthusiasm. 'You ain't got no chance! I'm gonna take Nicky all over Brooklyn when I get her back there. She don't know Brooklyn, not proper. She only kinda thinks she does. An' when she sees that bridge . . . '

Tex shut up the cross talk. He'd remembered something. 'Mahfra — it means Rain-in-Early-Summer — is sittin' back under a palm tree over there right now. You won't guess who's with her!'

They couldn't, so he told them. 'Louie the Camel!'

Elegant said, 'I'll kill that palooka when I see him.'

Rube said, 'You'd better not get him near me, Tex, I'm warnin' you.'

Only Dimmy said nothing, though he'd suffered more than any of them by the treachery of their comrade from the Bronx district of New York. Dimmy was too amiable to think of harsh things like vengeance. Perhaps that was why the Legion thought he was a bit dim, and had nicknamed him accordingly.

Tex just said tiredly, 'You won't touch him. That guy's suffered for all he did to us.' He told about the torture by those wild women in the desert. 'Just forget about what happened. Just let's get to a boat an' shake hands an' hope never to see a guy with a face like his ever again.'

They growled a bit, but Tex won his point. When he had finished arguing with them, he knew that Louie was safe.

They sat around then, relaxing. Tex was worried about the Arab girl and Louie. Louie wouldn't move far from that comparatively safe hiding place, of course, but Mahfra would get uneasy after a time, he felt certain, and would come down to look for him.

He didn't want her to come up to this barred window, because the *partizans* might be keeping close watch, and it was no help to them if Mahfra got into trouble, too. The local inhabitants would be particularly severe on the girl, because they didn't like to see their womenfolk on friendly terms with the infidel.

He was dragged out of his thoughts by Nicky's voice. She was saying, 'Why did that *partizan* betray you to the crowd, Tex?'

He looked at the girl. He had a respect for her intelligence. She sat at his feet, thinking, and looking mighty pretty at the same time, Tex thought.

'I mean, Tex, getting you bumped off by a mob in Bir Khula wouldn't put any dimes into a *partizan's* pocket, and they hunt men for the bounty they get for bringing in deserters' heads.'

'Meanin'?' The big cowboy from Texas hadn't cottoned on.

Nicky looked at him for a long moment. 'I'd say,' she guessed, 'that they're not interested in your head now, Tex, only in your death. I figger that Sturmer has told his men, 'Kill Legionnaire Texas — kill him or get him killed'. And he's promised a bounty bigger than they'd get for your head.'

'Meanin' that Sturmer's afraid to let me go alive?' Tex had bitten now. Then he looked at the girl's cameras, under a coat in a corner. 'I figger that goes for you too, honey — an' the boys. Sturmer doesn't want us to go outside tellin' the world he's hidin' in the French Foreign Legion. That makes us all in the same boat.'

'We must watch our step,' Nicky urged. 'From now on any one of us might be assassinated — anything to silence us.' She looked at Dimmy, lounging against the open window. 'I wouldn't stand there, Dimmy,' she urged. 'A man with a rifle could bump you off easily from the bushes over by the palm trees.'

Dimmy said, 'Aw, they wouldn't do a thing like that,' but he didn't convince himself, and he came away from the window.

Tex looked round. 'I figger Nicky's right, pards. Reckon we'd better keep our eyes skinned, even in prison, just in case of accidents.'

He looked at Elegant, who'd done rock-blasting in his time. Elegant was tapping the powder out of the rounds that Tex had given him earlier. He came to the last one and looked at the pile of dark, fine-grained powder in a heap before him.

He had a small empty tin that he'd scrounged from somewhere, and he shoved the powder in.

When that was done he squinted into the tin and then yapped, 'This powder ain't enough to blow a hole in a T'anks-givin' cake!'

8

Tex was on his feet in an instant. This put an end to their plans completely. He had no more rounds on him, 'brahim having taken his loaded gun.

He looked round. They were all looking at him in a startled manner — looking to him, he realized. He was their leader, and they depended upon his powers of resource.

He could only think, "brahim — or Mahfra!'

'brahim might be able to secure ammunition for them, but would they see him again before the night? If he were wise, he would keep well away from the prison, so as not to arouse suspicion of their escape plans.

Then — Mahfra? Would she come? Would it be safe if she did come? And could she get the ammunition from Louie if Tex did give her the instruction? For Louie spoke no Arabic, and the girl knew no English.

He stood at the window, gripping the bars and looking out. Burnoused men were hurrying across the waste lot towards the village centre. There was a low, humming sound coming from the village, the sound a large crowd makes when it is gathered together.

But Mahfra wasn't to be seen. They watched the sun decline, and they cursed their impotence, cursed the heat and the flies that came and pestered them. Only Nicky somehow kept her spirits. She tried to cheer them; if their plan to escape that night was now abortive, what did that signify? Wouldn't there be other nights? Wouldn't they have other chances?

Tex listened to those crowd noises. A man's high-pitched voice came faintly to their ears, as of one addressing a large audience in the open air. At times his voice was drowned by a deep-throated roar of approval. Tex listened, made guesses, but didn't say anything to his companions. There was no use in alarming them unnecessarily.

Up and down the room the men stalked, expressing their frustration in action, however limited it was. Nicky finally screamed, 'For the love of Pete, sit down. You give me the willies, wearing your feet out.'

Tex went again to the barred window, and looked gloomily out. All afternoon wide-eyed children had made pilgrimages to see the hated Franks at the barred window, but now they were going, as if afraid that dusk wouldn't give the safety over the evil eye that the hot, bright sun provided.

Gloomily Tex watched them go. There were lights from oil lamps, warm and yellow, showing now, mostly at cafés that were poorly patronized, perhaps because of that big meeting through the village. Night was descending rapidly. In a few hours 'brahim would be waiting for them, with swift horses that could carry them to safety out of this hostile Sahara.

And they would be cooped up inside this prison, incapable of taking advantage of the opportunity of escape.

It was galling, maddening. Tex found himself gripping the bars in fury, trying to wrest them from their sockets. He thought one moved slightly, tried again, and then decided it was imagination. No hope that way.

Then darkness came plunging down, swiftly, in tropical fashion. A yellow light gradually rose above the centre of the village, a light that seemed to dim and brighten alternately. Tex had seen such a light before — when a mob carried torches. That previous time, the mob had been in South Carolina, and they were on their way to a lynching.

Tex went cold at the thought, and turned to look at his companions, wondering if they suspected what he suspected. Dimmy had made himself comfortable and was snoring. Dimmy could do things like that. Rube and Elegant were just sitting with their backs to a wall, side by side and silent, shadowy figures whose faces showed as pale ovals in that near-blackness. Nicky, looking grey-white in her lighter clothes, was sitting just where she'd been before at Tex's feet.

They were all silent. Tex felt the despair that gripped them. He stayed where he was; at least the evening breeze through the barred window was soothing to his head and shoulders . . .

A hand touched his shoulder, lightly. He turned. Mahfra was standing there, her brown eyes big with terror. He was so close that he could see the quivering of those ripe red lips in spite of the darkening night.

She whispered, 'Oh, Takes, they are coming to kill you!'

Tex listened to the distant roaring of the crowd and knew what she meant. That roar was the loudest yet, and the most savage-sounding. He gripped her small hand that clutched the bars.

She was saying, 'I grew afraid, when you did not return. I came into the village and there heard that you had been taken prisoner. Oh, Takes. I have watched you for hours through this window and not dared to come to you because of watchers. Even now . . . '

Tex felt the others up on their feet, crowding round him. He saw those terrified eyes of the Arab maiden look from one shadowy face to another, but she did not run away.

The big Texan interrupted her. 'Mahfra, we plan to escape this night. Run back to Louie and get from him all the spare ammunition he's got. We need it to blow a hole in this wall.'

Mahfra wailed softly. 'It is very far. They are planning to come and drag you from the jail and cut off your heads. Oh, Takes, I shall be too late, and I love you!'

Tex took her by the slim wrists. 'Go, Mahfra. Run as you've never run before. They may take time. Perhaps you can save us yet.'

She hesitated. Then it seemed to Tex that she began to gather up her strength and courage, and suddenly she went running off into the darkness.

Tex turned. He was thinking, 'It'll take her twenty minutes at least.' That was, if Louie were co-operative and didn't sit on that ammunition. He might think it all a trick to render him helpless.

Twenty minutes — then time for Elly to make the bomb and plant it. Half an hour. That was a long time. In half an hour that mob could have stormed the prison and dragged them out to their death. The guards, he thought contemptuously, weren't likely to try to protect their charges. He knew mobs, too, and knew it would be useless now for the sheik to try to use his influence to stop them; night covered men's faces, so that they could do things, anonymously without thought to a reckoning with their elders later.

Rube said, 'What was all that?' And Tex interpreted. But he didn't tell them of Mahfra's last words.

Rube whistled. 'I saw the dame. Them eyes!'

'Them teeth,' whistled Elly. 'You sure pick 'em, Tex.'

Nicky said, coldly, 'Don't mind me. I'm not the jealous kind.' Then, generously, she squeezed Tex's arm and said, 'She looked very lovely, Tex. You get all the girls to fall for you, don't you?'

Tex said, 'It's the gypsy in me,' and then sat down to await the Arab girl's return.

The mob came before that. Nicky was at the window, watching. Suddenly she called out a warning. They all crowded round her. Looking over her fair hair, Tex saw a mob spilling out from many alleyways on to the waste lot before them. They had torches, as he had suspected, and the red, leaping glow fell on excited, glistening faces.

As is the way with mobs, having got so far, they all stopped and shouted, and then men stood before them and made speeches, inflaming them to the desired state of madness. One of the speakers was quite near. Tex looked at him, trying to identify him in that shifting red light. He wasn't certain, but he thought it could be the *partizan* who had betrayed him to the Arabs.

He thought, 'Maybe there's a lot of *partizans* in that crowd, stirrin' up trouble.' Could be they were acting on instructions from their ex-Nazi leader. If the mob destroyed the prisoners, then Sturmer would feel that much safer.

He looked at his luminous-dialled watch. It was over twenty minutes since Mahfra had gone. Uneasily he thought, 'This mob's scared her off. She won't dare come to the window with this crowd facin' us.' Or perhaps Louie was holding on to that precious ammunition.

Nicky turned, her face very close to his. She whispered, 'I don't think your girl friend's going to make it.'

Tex put his arm across those slim, warm shoulders so soft to the touch under her white silk blouse. 'Then die happy,' he cracked. 'She ain't my gal friend. Just an admirer.' He wished he hadn't said that immediately. It sounded crude. He hadn't meant it literally . . .

The mob was surging forward again. The roar of their voices was so deafening that when the prisoners spoke to each other now they had to shout.

Elly shouted, 'We're sunk, Tex. That gal cain't get t'rough now even if she wants.'

He jerked away from the window, yelping with pain. There was blood coming from his flattened nose. Something had crashed against his face, something heavy that had fallen to the ground with a thud.

Rube shouted, 'Keep away from the window. The damn' so-and-so's are

169

throwing stones!'

They pulled aside from the danger area, but still continued to watch that advancing mob. Tex hadn't given up hope of Mahfra and was still watching. He moved towards the window again, risking injury, so desperate was he now to see the girl who could save their lives. The milling mob was no more than forty yards away.

His fists clenching savagely, he turned at last, hope gone. Mahfra couldn't help them. Nothing could help them. In a few moments they would be fighting for their lives. And Nicky . . . He stopped thinking when he came to Nicky in his thoughts.

His foot kicked against something solid as he changed his position. He didn't think about it. He moved again. He kicked it again. That stone that had made Elly bleed, he was thinking. Then suddenly he was down on his hands and knees, frantically searching.

For stones don't make dull, metallic sounds when kicked.

The others were standing back, wondering what he was doing, groping on the floor in the dark. He rose. He was holding something. He shouted, 'Elly, Mahfra did it. Here's a bundle of rifle cartridges. Get movin', fellar!'

There was a crash on the prison door at that. Evidently the guards were letting the mob do it the hard way and hadn't surrendered the keys. But the door wouldn't stand up long to an attack of that sort.

Rube was striking matches, kneeling. Elly was working frantically, digging open the cartridges and emptying them. But everything else was ready. Within minutes he'd packed that tin with explosive powder and had it shoved into a hole that he had been patiently grouting out of the wall for days. The tin fitted tightly.

Elly pushed on the lid. He'd made a simple detonator, which passed through the lid. Then he put a plug of dried mud carefully over the lid. A nail was fixed into the plug, its point touching the detonator.

The outside door crashed. The fevered shrieks of the blood-maddened crowd intensified as they poured into the prison house. Tex and Rube ran to the door that led into the hall. It had no lock, no bolts, or bars. They put their big boots as wedges against the bottom. That would hold the door until the crowd brought up a battering ram.

Elly worked feverishly. He fixed everything in position, and then told them to stand back. Rube and Tex couldn't. The mob was already searching the other rooms. Then they found this closed door, and the prisoners heard the excited voices only a couple of inches from their ears. The mob began to push on the door. Rube and Tex braced — and held it.

Elly stood on one side and hit the protruding end of the nail in the plug of mud with a piece of stick. Nothing happened. The mob began to throw its weight against the door. Tex and Rube straining to hold them, felt their feet slip an inch.

Elly smacked it again. And again it didn't fire. The mob threw itself in fury upon that door, and again it gave. A hand came experimentally round the door edge. Nicky ran across and smacked it with the flat of her hand — hard, and it hurt. The fingers withdrew.

Elly was swearing frantically to himself. He swung again and now he'd given up hope. That damn' nail wasn't opposite the detonator cap for all his careful work . . .

Elly was blown on to his back. The room seemed to sway under the impact of that crashing sound. In the hallway outside, there was a sudden silence from the crowd and the pressure on the door eased momentarily.

Tex and Rube were flattened against the door. Their ears were ringing.

Dazed, recovering from the shock of that explosion in such a confined space, they looked towards the wall.

After all that, there was no hole in it.

It wasn't easy to see, with all that swirling dust from the concussion of the blast within the room, and the cordite smoke that blew out with the explosion. Together it almost blotted out even the faint light of early night.

But if a hole had been blown in the wall, Tex knew there would nave been a big through draught, and they would have felt it.

He saw the dim shape of Elly moving

against the wall. Elly called to Dimmy, and the two men began to work frantically. Rube shouted in agony, 'What gives Elly?'

'There's a great crack in the wall. We c'n knock a hole t'rough.' Elly was gasping from the exertion.

The crowd recovered itself in the hallway. The noise grew to pandemonium, and again weight was thrown on that door. Rube and Tex fought with all their might to give their comrades the minutes they needed to clear a way through that broken wall.

Then the air began to feel cleaner. Holding that door they realized that a hole was growing in the broken mud wall.

Then Elly crawled out into the night. He shouted, but they didn't know what he said. Dimmy was busy stuffing the girl through the opening now. She was dragging her precious photographic equipment with her. Tex saw Dimmy wriggle his heavy body through the opening.

'You next,' he gritted. 'I'll hold 'em for a few seconds on my own.'

Fists were battering the door, then this gave way to a regular rhythmic shove on the part of many shoulders that was much harder to hold back. Tex felt himself slipping. Sweating from the exertion, trying desperately to hold his sliding foot braced against that door, he saw Rube run across and stoop to get through the hole. He seemed to take an awful long time.

The door was half a foot open, suddenly. Hands were swinging round, trying to get at him. They found his head and began to buffet it, and he could do nothing to protect himself. Another mighty shove and there was almost enough room for a man to squeeze through. A man was coming in. Rube's feet were disappearing.

Tex jumped. He cracked the chin that was showing round the corner of the door, then dived headlong into the hole in the wall.

Probably the darkness saved him. Probably it took a few vital seconds before the crowd, pouring in a wild flood into the room, saw that hole low down in the wall, and the white trousered legs wriggling through it.

Tex felt strong hands grasp his arms and begin to drag him into the cooler night air that felt so fresh and sweet after the dust-and-cordite stink in their prison. He was being dragged through, swiftly — and then hands grasped his booted ankles and held him.

It became a tug-of-war for a couple of seconds, with Tex as the rope, part way through that thick mud wall. Then somehow he got one foot free and kicked out. His heel must have caught someone and hurt. The next moment he was released at his ankles, and he came out on to his friends with a rush.

They dragged him to his feet, and started him at a staggering run across the open ground behind the jail. He didn't know where he was going, and why, but the others seemed to have some idea.

He saw shadowy white figures pouring round the corner of the dark building to his right.

Then they were among bushes, under the shadows of the tall palms. And he got the smell of horseflesh.

Nicky was already in a saddle. The others were leaping up. The mob was racing at their heels now, howling savagely at being deprived of its prey. An Arab came out of the gloom.

He had a curiously pale face in that poor light and was a stranger to Tex. But he spoke with the voice of 'brahim. 'Mount, Takes!'

Tex needed no second bidding. He leapt into the saddle as the others spurred away. The Arab vaulted on to another mount and came thundering beside him. Then the Arab moved forward and took the lead.

Within minutes they were out of the oasis and into the bare desert beyond. At that the Arab slowed to a walk and the others all gathered round him. They were exultant. Elly was slapping everyone on the back and chanting, 'We made it. Boy oh boy, we bust outa the cooler!'

Reaction at saving their lives, almost when the mob was upon them, gripped them in a form of hysteria for a moment.

Tex found himself hugging the girl, and

then someone else grabbed her and did a bit of hugging.

But in time they cooled down and became practical. They did not fear discovery sitting there in the desert, because the night was too dark for their tracks to be followed, and the Sahara was a big place to search.

Then Tex made a discovery. He'd shoved his face close up to that Arab's. It was a clean-shaven Arab. But he spoke again with the voice of 'brahim, laughing.

'It's me, Takes. Do you not know your old friend, 'brahim?'

Tex said, 'Wal, what do you know? The boy's gone an' shaved hissel'. Now, why?'

'brahim told him. 'I am tired of the desert. I go with you to America. There I hope to marry Nicky.'

Tex said, heartily, 'I'm with you right up to the last sentence, brother. We'll get you to America if you'll just help us outa this goddamned desert.'

Then he remembered he had business to do before that — and then remembered something else.

Mahfra and Louie.

He told them, 'You stay here. Louie an' Mahfra's got to be rounded up.'

There was a bit of argument after that. Rube said, what the heck, he couldn't go risking his life back in the oasis on account of a heel like Louie the Camel. Goldam it, the fellar was the cause of all their trouble, wasn't he? And 'brahim murmured, 'The girl — she is peasant, of no account.'

'Okay,' said Tex. 'you go on without me. But I'm not leavin' 'em in that oasis.'

Angrily he wheeled his mount, looking at the stars for guidance. So then 'brahim rode up beside him 'brahim would be able to find his way even in this dark, and he didn't think Tex would.

Tex's anger subsided. It evaporated completely when he made the belated discovery that a Lebel rifle was in the saddle boot, and ammunition in the pocket. 'brahim had equipped them well for the long trail across the desert to the coast. He was a good friend.

They approached the east end of the oasis with caution. In the distance they could still hear the sound of voices, as if the crowd were gathered together and unwilling to disperse. But that was in the distance.

They rode in among the trees as near to where Louie and Mahfra had been as Tex could estimate, but it seemed a hopeless task to try to find them.

So Tex did a bold thing. He rode on the desert edge within a couple of yards of the sprawling scrub vegetation and called quite loudly, 'Mahfra — Louie!'

It seemed an eternity before an answer came from the dark bushes. Then he heard sounds, and some were made by nervous horses; forms loomed up out of the darkness — Mahfra and Louie, leading their two mounts.

Tex swung out of his saddle. Mahfra recognized his tall form and flew into his arms. She had had a bad night and was shaking with terror. Tex spoke in Arabic — 'You saved us, Mahfra. For that my everlasting thanks.'

Louie grasped him by the hand and shook it as if he would never finish. Plainly his nerves were as raw as Mahfra's.

'She couldn't explain what had happened to you, but I knew it was bad,' Louie told him, his voice breaking with relief. 'What happened?'

Tex said, 'It can wait. Get mounted. We've got to be well into the desert before the moon comes up.'

Mahfra objected to riding a mount separately; she wanted to sit up in front of Tex, but he wasn't having that. So he settled things by lifting her and sitting her on one of the horses then he mounted and led her horse by the reins.

'brahim made no mistake. Without mishap he led them back to where the other quartet waited. Now that there were eight of them, six armed, it felt quite a strong posse, and it was with lighter spirits that they set off south-eastwards.

At first they went slowly, taking it in turns to lead the way, the leader testing the ground on foot. But when the moon rose and showed clearly any obstacles in their path, they all mounted and set off at a good pace. For a while they swapped stories, and then silence fell on them.

Tex kept them going all night, save for

one brief pause shortly before dawn, when they drank sparingly of water and ate some of the food that 'brahim had packed into their saddlebags. Even when the sun was up, he would not slacken the pace. Out here on the comparatively flat desert they were sitting targets for any large group of men, and he wanted to get into the hills that 'brahim talked of, where strategy could prevail and possibly help them.

And always at the back of his mind was the thought of his mission to Africa — the capture of ex-Nazi General Sturmer. He was still determined not to leave the country without completing his task.

When the blazing sun was up and the heat came reflecting off the hot sand in shimmering waves of turbulent air, he looked back at their tracks. They were plain to see, reaching back to the horizon that was formed by a smooth-rounded sandhill. A man would need to be blind not to be able to follow such a trail.

The *partizans* weren't blind, he was thinking. They'd find and follow this trail, even if the Bir Khula Arabs didn't. That was their profession, following deserters' trails. And Sturmer would come along with them.

The thought satisfied him.

He looked ahead. Distantly, many miles away, he could see the ragged shape of barren, sun-bleached mountains. He felt that not until they ran into them, into that barrier between them and Libya, would they have safety — even then it would be mighty little safety, he was thinking.

He kept looking back, all that morning, but they saw no sign of pursuit. Just before the sickeningly hot sun was at its zenith, he gave the order to halt. The horses were jaded and needed rest, anyway, and they might just as well take advantage of the moment to rest themselves.

He sent Rube to keep watch from the nearest hill. Then they sat around, ate and drank, rested as well as the sun would let them — and talked,

Mahfra had taken her place at Tex's feet. She was at ease now with the members of the party, confident because she had her 'Takes' with her, yet she looked at the lovely blonde American girl speculatively. She couldn't speak English, hadn't ever been out of the desert, but she could recognize competition when she saw it.

Nicky had been very sweet to her, but that cut no ice where a girl thought her prospects were in danger.

Nicky said, now, 'She's a nice girl, Tex.' 'brahim was listening. He looked at the Arab girl indifferently. To him a sheik's son, she was of inferior caste and not to be considered. Tex saw the look. He also noted how white the Arab's fresh-shaven chin looked. All morning they had joked with the Arab about shaving off his beard because Nicky had said she liked men without hair on their faces, and he had taken it in good part.

Tex said, 'What's on yow mind?' — bluntly.

Nicky looked at nails that seemed to have been recently manicured. 'Oh, I'm just thinking, Tex. I mean, what's going to happen to her when you reach America?'

He knew what she was thinking. It was going to be hard to get into that pretty

Arab head the fact that Tex didn't have any amorous intentions towards her. It was all right the girl deciding that she was his, but Tex didn't want her. He liked her, was deeply grateful to her, but it was a Western custom to love a girl before taking her as a wife. Mahfra wouldn't know about such things. She had accepted that she was Tex's because the big ex-Legionnaire had carried her away from her home. In her own tribe there could be only one end to such conduct — she would naturally become the wife of the man.

Tex sprawled back on the sand, his kepi over his face. Nicky was astonished to hear him drawl, 'Oh, Mahfra? Don't you worry none about her. That gal's got money in her own right — plenty of dough.'

'She has?' Nicky was startled. Then she realized that one grey eye of the big Legionnaire was watching the effect of his words upon 'brahim. 'brahim was looking at the Arab maiden with much greater interest now.

'Sure she has. You know what, Nicky,

she's got land in Texas so big you could fit Bir Khula into it a couple of thousand times. Yeah, an' when the round-up comes, there's ten thousand head o' cattle bawlin' their heads off right outside the purtiest ranch you ever saw in all your life. My, my, but the fellar that marries that gal's goin' to be a lucky man. He won't have to worry none for the rest of his days.' Nicky looked at him — and caught on. She didn't know though, that big, generous Tex, who knew they owed their lives to the bravery of this girl, who had risked death before that mob by hurling that ammunition in to them in prison — Nicky wasn't to know that Tex had just given his dead brother's ranch to the girl as a marriage dowry. He had enough with his own vast lands, anyway.

She whispered, for only Tex to hear, 'You're a good guy, Tex.'

That other eye came from under the kepi. 'You c'n say that agen, Nicky,' he told her. There was humour in his eyes — and more, as he looked at her.

They lay there under a sun that tried to fry them, faces within inches of each other. Their eyes met and held. Nicky whispered, 'You don't know New York, do you, Tex?'

He shook his head. She was looking at the muscles in his strong face, was thinking, 'This man's a fighter, a man any girl could be proud of.'

Aloud she said, 'It's not a good place to live in, Tex. You're kind of crowded on top of each other. You wouldn't like it at all.'

Blue eyes demurely dropped. 'I've always hankered after a life in more open country — like Texas, for instance.'

There was no one to see. Tex's hand stole out and gently took her's. 'You wanna come down to Texas,' he whispered. 'Come an' stay with me, say.'

Nicky's eyes opened in mock alarm. 'What, an unmarried woman? Shame on you for the suggestion, Legionnaire Texas!'

Tex just grinned and said, 'You know, Texas sure has got everythin', parsons too. Maybe he could fix things for us, huh?'

She whispered, 'Maybe,' And then they just lay and looked at each other.

Elly got up and started to climb the hill so as to relieve Rube. There wasn't much difference, so far as comfort was concerned, lying under the sun on top of that hill, or lying under the sun at the foot of it. All the same, Elly felt it comradely to share the watch.

Tex looked up at the movement. His eye caught another movement 'brahim, the sheik's son, was surreptitiously passing a slice of melon across to an astonished but delighted Mahfra. More, he was looking at the pretty Arab girl in a very kindly way.

Tex lay back and smiled contentedly. He felt that he was working himself nicely out of what might have become a very embarrassing position.

Lovely, fair-haired Nicky saw the smile and asked softly, 'What's tickling you, big boy?'

But Tex just shook his head and wouldn't answer. An hour later Louie the Camel staggered to his feet and began to climb the hill towards Elly. Tex called, 'Where are you going?'

Louie shrugged. 'I figger I got to do my

turn of watchin' same as anyone else,' he called back. He looked an ugly figure, bent because of his bruised body, his clothes torn from the manhandling he'd received, and with his long yellow, camel's teeth protruding.

The other men hadn't spoken to him since he joined the party. Louie knew he didn't deserve friendliness, but a man can't live by himself. This gesture of his, to take his turn on watch, was an effort to win friendliness, Tex knew. But he also knew that Louie was in no condition to climb that hill: for days he would have to nurse his strength, otherwise he would collapse on them.

So he rose. 'I figger it's my turn,' he said, and he wouldn't listen to any arguments.

Louie went back to sit with the party, while Tex slowly climbed the hill. His feet sank in over the boot tops, so that it was an effort to walk, and it took him a long time to gain the summit.

When he was near to the top, he paused for breath, and wiped the sweat out of his eyes with the back of his hand.

Elly was lying huddled there, his back to the sun.

Tex began to climb again. Three or four paces. Then again he stopped, and this time his head jerked up to look at that figure on the skyline.

Instinct told Tex that the Legionnaire from Brooklyn was too still. He shouted. Legionnaire Joe Ellighan didn't move.

Tex thought, 'God, how long's he been like that?' And he began to climb as fast as he could go.

When he reached Elly, the flat-faced warrior from Brooklyn was stirring. Tex saw those small brown eyes open dully. They looked at Tex, then jerked wide open with alarm. Then they looked over his shoulder.

Tex looked,, westward, too. He saw Sturmer and his *partizans* within a couple of hundred yards of them, right at the foot of this swelling mound of sand.

9

Tex went flat on his face, dragging Elly with him. Then he began to scramble frantically backwards, down off the summit of the hill.

He was praying, 'Don't look this way, you damn' head-hunters. Just keep doin' what you're doin'!'

As they crabbed backwards through the sand, their eyes never left that party below. Tex whispered, 'We had a bit of luck that time, Elly.'

For while Elly had slept on watch, wearied by a night and morning in the saddle, Captain Herman Sturmer and his *partizans* had ridden to within a few hundred yards of them — and then had called a halt.

That had been luck, luck such as they could never hope to have again. For if Sturmer and his renegades had ridden just another two hundred yards, they would have surprised the sleeping Elly, and seen their quarry resting at the foot of the hill.

But the *partizans* must have ridden at a cracking pace, to have come so far since daylight, and there comes a time when horse if not rider must be rested. Fortunately for Tex's party, rest had become imperative just in time.

Once below the skyline, both rose to their feet and began to race madly down towards their companions. Tex heard Elly gasp, 'Oh, god, Tex, I oughta be shot for that! Sleepin'. I don't know what I was doin'.'

Tex just grinned and said, 'You got away with it, brother — we all got away with it. They might rest for hours, an' we can be miles away by the time they mount again.'

Their comrades came climbing to their feet as the pair raced up, alarm on their faces. Tex called, 'Pack up — get movin'. Sturmer's mob's just over the skyline!'

Louie was first in the saddle, injured though he was. Louie had been at close quarters with the *partizans*, and he never wanted to be within reach of their sword hands again.

Desperately they raced to stow water bottles and food into their saddlebags. Then they mounted, got into line and began the journey again to those distant jagged peaks, which were their goal.

They kept looking back, and with every minute that they travelled without sight of pursuers, their relief grew. Finally Tex brought the horses down to a walk again. Their lives might depend upon the stamina of these beasts, and their strength must be husbanded accordingly.

The big American sat round in his saddle, eyes narrowed to face the glare of the high-riding sun. He marvelled at their escape. 'I even shouted to waken Elly, an' they never heard it,' he kept saying.

Nobody said an unkind thing to their companion who had nearly cost them their lives. It was something that could happen to all of them, they knew, and they knew besides that they owed their escape from the prison house to Elly because he alone had known how to make an explosive charge.

Half an hour after resuming their journey, when they were within five or six miles of the first of the foothills, they ran onto the trail of other horsemen.

It was a recent trail, too, they could tell, because the sand around the hoofmarks was still slowly falling in. Could be no more than an hour or so old, Tex thought. In silence they rode alongside those tracks, examining them. After a while Tex came to a conclusion.

'There's about six in this party,' he said aloud. His eyes were on those approaching hills, ugly and barren, the life burnt out of them by this almost incessant sunshine.

Rube knew what he was thinking. 'It's Ca-ca an' his boyos?'

'It's Ca-ca,' Tex said grimly. He was pretty certain there'd be no other party of six in this vicinity.

'Looks like they've got the same idea as we have,' Rube growled, looking anxiously ahead. The way north was closed by the French armies; south-east to the Libyan coast seemed the only way of escape from the Sahara Desert.

This complicated things. Now they were between two lots of ruthless enemies — vicious renegades ahead, who would shoot them because they hated them, and the head-hunting *partizans* close on their heels.

Riding steadily towards those hills, beginning to climb now, Tex thought how exposed they were, how for certain they must be seen by anyone climbing within those mountains. And renegades were men who always looked back.

About four in the afternoon, when they were so dry in their mouths that they could hardly speak, they entered a long, winding defile that led through the mountains. Before them and on either side rose the grim rocky peaks, dark red where the sun reflected on them — grimly, forbiddingly black in the shadows. It seemed to Nicky, the newspaper-woman, that this was a tortured land, that it writhed and twisted into fantastic shapes before it had become stilled forever. Everywhere were great rock formations, and the defile was never straight for more than fifty yards at once, and small valleys had been rent in its sides, offering perfect cover for ambushers.

That was what came to Tex's mind, slowly riding, sometimes in shadow, sometimes in blazing sunshine, up that cleft in the mountains. He was thinking, 'If anyone looked back an' saw it, it would just naturally occur to them to lay for us.' Ca-ca would jump at the chance to settle old scores.

At the head of a steep climb, they looked back over the desert they had just left. Nicky was alongside Tex. She suddenly gripped his arm — she was pointing.

They all looked.

A tiny cloud of dust rose from the desert, four or five miles away. As they watched, it blew away and revealed a large party of white-robed men on horses.

Nobody spoke. Nobody needed to. This would be ex-Nazi General Herman Sturmer hard on their heels. The chase was on again.

Tex turned his horse into the defile again. They had paused to rest on a shelf that ran out of the mountainside. The moment he got his mount on to the barely discernible trail, the animal died under him.

Tex felt the mount rear and then begin to collapse. And then an echoing sound came ringing down between those high rock walls — the crack of a rifle.

Tex jumped clear of his dying, kicking horse, dragging his Lebel out of the saddleboot as he did so. He was yelling, 'Back under cover,' as he did so, diving for that shelf at the same time.

He landed on all fours right under the feet of their startled horses. The men were swinging off, all except Louie, who was too stiff to get out of his saddle. Rube and Elly were down on their faces, watching up the defile. Rube saw a movement and ripped off a shot that shattered the silence of the mountains. A volley came back.

Tex went worming his way alongside the men. 'They've got us trapped, though they don't know it,' he was saying. If they rode out on to the trail they would be under fire from the renegade Legionnaires; if they stayed where they were on that exposed shelf, they would be sitting targets for the *partizans* when they rode into the foothills.

Tex saw a series of movements up the defile. Ca-ca and his men were moving into positions where they could cover the trail completely. They must have felt in a good position, able to take their time in this little war. For there could only be one end to it, and that soon, in this land where a man lives as long as his water bottle was filled. Soon Tex and his party would be driven from cover to risk death in a hail of bullets because of the maddening thirst that must come to them. True, Ca-ca's waterbottles would be emptying, but they could lie in selected places in the shade, and would not feel the effects of the sun anywhere near as much as those on an exposed shelf.

Nicky crawled up. She had been watching over the edge of the shelf, back towards the approaching *partizans*.

'They're coming along fast, Tex,' she whispered. 'Any more firing and they'll hear it and will be warned of our position.'

So Tex told his companions not to fire unless they had to. The longer Sturmer and his renegades were in ignorance of their plight, the better.

He rolled back and stared around him. What he saw didn't inspire him with much hope. Rube crawled back. He was grinning, though Tex couldn't see what there was to feel cheerful about.

He growled, sourly, 'What'n heck's tickled you, brother?'

Rube licked dry lips with an equally dry tongue. His voice was a croak when he spoke. 'I c'n see horses way up the defile,' he said. 'Just see the tops of their heads an' their ears at times.'

Tiredly Tex said, 'So what?'

Rube was looking at the steep slope at the north end of this shelf upon which they rested. 'I was thinkin' — it'd be a helluva thing if we could sneak aroun', get on their hosses, an' leave 'em to fight it out with Sturmer.'

Tex looked at him for a long moment, then let his eyes turn to the end of the shelf where Rube was looking. Dimmy and Louie were listening, Louie still up on his horse. 'brahim had taken Rube's place alongside Elly. Tex noticed that Mahfra was squatting at the feet of the sheik's son, ready to reload his rifle, which was the way among Arab women-folk.

Nicky's quick brain saw the possibilities. She threw her voice into urging Tex to risk it. 'Rube's idea's not so silly as it sounds,' she said quickly.

'It means abandoning our horses.' They didn't know it, but Tex's brain was considering another plan, too.

'What odds if we take theirs? They've got six beasts, and they'll carry eight of us all right.'

Rube said, 'Look, Tex, we c'n climb right up behind them, out of sight the whole way. They'll never know until we go ridin' away on their horses.'

Tex said, 'It'll be a terrible climb,' but he'd made up his mind to encourage the scheme. They'd only be shot down like sitting pheasants, exposed there on the shelf, when the *partizans* came round that corner below them.

'We'll make it,' said Nicky.

They weren't waiting for formal decisions now. All were moving hastily away from the defile end of the rock shelf on which they stood. Dimmy good-naturedly gave Louie a hand down out of the saddle. Louie's face was ghastly. He could only stand with difficulty.

They began to move across to where some sort of foothold was offered over the shoulder of this hill that backed the shelf. Elegant cracked, 'Rube the Schemer! Where'd we be but for him?'

Tex said, 'Sleepin' it out on some comfortable barrack-room bed somewhere, maybe.' But Rube knew he was thankful for the idea that had come to his fertile mind.

They all stood and looked up at the path they had to follow. Rain had worn a way down the rock face, making a channel only a few feet wide and so steep that it seemed to rise vertically above them. But there were footholds, and with courage they knew they could climb it. What lay beyond they didn't know, but Rube kept saying, 'We'll find a way of workin' round 'em an' keepin' out of

201

sight all the time.'

He was rubbing his hands and chuckling, those blue eyes of his sparkling with delight. He was thinking, 'Boy, oh boy, that Ca-ca's face when we ride off with their hosses!' He didn't like the sallow-faced Ca-ca, and consequently he was delighted to put one across the renegade.

Tex stood back; he was thinking furiously, looking at the awful climb before his companions, and then watching the approaching riders now only a mile or so away on the dazzlingly bright desert far below.

Abruptly, at a moment when Rube was already beginning to draw himself up the rainwater channel, they heard Tex's voice.

'You go on without me.'

Tex caught the catch in Nicky's breath. She turned and looked at him, her blue eyes big and frightened — fearing for him. He looked at her and thought how thin her face had gone, how brown her skin was turning from their day out on the desert trail. But she looked lovely, for all her tiredness.

Deliberately he avoided her eyes when he spoke again.

'I came to this darned country for a purpose — to get that Nazi Sturmer an' take him back to stand trial for his war crimes. Waal, I reckon to do just that.'

His hand waved towards the desert, hundreds of feet below them. 'There's Sturmer. I'm goin' to meet him. You go through an' get them hosses. When you've got 'em, keep watch on the trail an' — waal, maybe you'll be able to help me, that's all I figger.'

He shrugged. He couldn't detail any plan, because he had only the glimmerings of a hazardous idea in his own mind. He didn't think much to it, didn't think he stood much chance of surviving. But then it had been like that all during these days that he had been on the run from the Legion. Facing death was becoming a habit with him lately.

They didn't try to talk him out of the idea. They knew him too well by now to attempt it. When this big Texas said, 'That's what I'm gonna do,' that's what he did.

Rube looked down, nodded briefly and began to climb that channel. Dimmy followed, finding nimbleness in his heavy limbs because his life depended on it. Nicky came after the ex-Legionnaires; when she'd got up a yard or so, she turned and held out her hand to help Mahfra. Mahfra smiled. They were friends now.

Then 'brahim followed, and then it was Louie's turn. Elegant yapped, 'C'mon, Bronx boy. Show'm how to do it.'

They'd known that Louie was ill, suffering from long-riding in the saddle after that torture by the Arab women, but until now they hadn't realized how badly he was hurt. They saw a white face, eyes unnaturally big and bright, saw the slack jaw and noted the quick, panting breath.

Louie said, 'You'd better go without me, fellars. I'm about through. I'd never climb that damn' mountain.'

Elly looked at Tex, quickly. Then he became falsely hearty. 'Sure you c'n make it, Louie. Anything a Brooklyn fellar c'n do, you c'n do. C'mon, let's go.'

Louie slumped, first on to his knees

and then on to his seat. He said, 'It ain't no use, fellars. That ride's killed me.' He looked at them. Once he had given them over to the enemy. Now they were looking concerned at him, forgetting what he had done.

He said, 'You're a coupla good guys. Look after yourself.'

The two ex-Legionnaires looked at each other. Tex said, 'You go, Elly. Louie's right; he'll never make it.'

The big, pug-faced son of Brooklyn turned reluctantly and began to climb. A couple of yards up he hesitated, then said, 'Look, I'll carry Louie on my back . . . '

Tex shook his head. 'You'd never make it, not up that blamed mountain. On your way, fellar,' Then he looked at Louie. He said, 'You're right, Louie. An' now I must leave you. I'll do what I can to help you, but . . . '

But there wasn't anything he could do, he was thinking. He looked down on to the desert. He'd have to hurry. The *partizans* were entering the defile now. He lowered himself over the edge of the cliff. His eyes rested on Louie.

There was despair on that poor, white, tortured face. The burning, feverish eyes told of the terror in the man's soul — the fear of being deserted by his companions in this hell on earth, surrounded by enemies, and knowing it had to be if they were to save their own lives.

Tex couldn't look at Louie the Camel for long. He just nodded and then let himself go.

He went sliding down that steep slope, at first with toes stubbing and hands clutching to control his speed. Then some obstruction threw him sideways, and he ended the journey in a slow, horizontal roll.

He ended up in a pocket of sand at the foot of the cliff, and apart from a few grazes his descent had done him no harm. He rose, turned, and started running. He got over a neck of rock and dropped into a dry wadi beyond that emptied into the defile.

He ran to where the wadi joined up with the defile. He was now several hundred yards below the shelf on which stood their horses — and Louie.

Almost at once the *partizans* came trotting round the rocky trail, Sturmer at their head. Tex crouched out of sight behind a big rock. But his eyes never left his enemy.

Sturmer, in his accustomed outfit of blue Legion officer's uniform with Arab headdress, looked out of place among those savage-looking Arab renegades, those hunters of the Legion deserters — headhunters!

He looked slight, and the rimless eyeglasses that he wore gave him a clerkish appearance. His face had the sallow thinness that a solicitor might have, long immured in sunless chambers, and yet Sturmer was a man who lived his life in the saddle.

An unprepossessing man, yet Tex wasn't deceived by appearances. He knew that mercy could more easily be expected at the hands of these bearded, burnoused renegades than from the man who had been a high-rankmg German afficer in the desert war of the 1940's.

Sturmer didn't know the meaning of the word mercy.

The *partizans* had ridden past where Tex lay hidden, when suddenly one of them called out sharply and pointed. At once the whole party reined, and guns lifted.

They had seen the horses high up on that rock shelf.

Some of the *partizans* at once dismounted and began to go up the defile at the run, guns pressed to their sides in readiness for action. Tex stood up at that in agony, praying that his companions would be far enough up that channel to be out of sight now. He was relieved to find that he couldn't see anyone, not even Louie on the shelf. Louie must have gone down on his face hard back against the cliff wall.

A *partizan* suddenly jumped out on to the trail, danced for a second and then fell face downwards. Almost immediately afterwards, the sound of a rifle shot crackled down the narrow defile. Tex looked up. A plume of smoke was drifting high up the mountainside.

Ca-ca's mob had opened fire on the Arab.

10

At once there was a flurry of activity as men raced their mounts under cover and then leapt off and began firing up to where the Legionnaire renegades lay. The return fire was furious and almost incessant. Evidently Ca-ca and his men had recognized the *partizans*. Their grim glee at having trapped Tex's party must have changed to horror at the unexpected sight of those thirty *partizans* cantering up the trail.

Now, thought Tex with some satisfaction, they would be in an unholy panic; for at sight of those renegade Arabs riding alongside Sturmer, they must have known their heads were in jeopardy.

He began to run forward. Sturmer alone hadn't dismounted. Instead he had cantered his rearing, nervous horse backwards, and now, sitting to the rear of his men, he was examining the enemy positions through field glasses.

Tex's pulse was racing. This was something better than he had hoped for. Hugging cover all the way, he glided from rock to rock up the defile, approaching his enemy from the rear. The battle raged, Ca-ca and his men hurling lead as fast as they could load, high up there in the winding defile.

Once Tex glanced at the rock shelf where their nervous horses were standing huddled against the cliff wall. He saw no sign of Louie, but that signified nothing. He might have been spotted and shot, of course, but Tex had an idea he would be crouched down on his face, out of sight. Probably the *partizans* didn't even suspect his presence; probably they thought that these horses were the mounts of the party firing at them from up the valley.

Sturmer began to shout in Arabic to his men. Tex, almost behind him, got the drift of what he was calling. He had recognized the men for deserters and he was shouting, '*Mes arabis*, there are six above you who can lose their heads — six bounties you can gather, for they are Legion deserters!'

It was like tempting hungry wolves with raw, red meat. Tex felt the change in atmosphere; it was as if the place became charged with wild savagery. Now nothing would stop those dogs of headhunters in their efforts to get at their victims, he thought. He watched them go moving forward, firing as they went, taking risks now in their eagerness to get those heads.

Tex was within fifteen yards of Sturmer, that slight man in blue Legion uniform and Arab headdress. He had made his plans. They must include Louie. Louie couldn't be left to die. He looked up the defile, but couldn't see the horses of the six renegade Legionnaires. He prayed that his companions would have scaled that awful mountainside and reached a position of safety behind the unconscious renegades. He knew, anyway, that they hadn't been detected in the act of climbing, for otherwise there would have been firing before the *partizans'* arrival.

Probably the sight of those fierce, hooded Arabs had absorbed all their attention, so that none had been looking for a possible enemy climbing round their flank.

Tex got so far in his thoughts, then he began to run forward. His heart was in his mouth, for if Sturmer turned while he was covering that open ground, he, Tex, would be a dead man.

Sturmer did start to turn, but he began the movement too late. Tex was in the act of leaping up over the horse's haunches when startled eyes looked round at him from behind flashing eyeglasses.

Sturmer's mouth opened to yell; his hand stabbed down to draw his revolver from his holster.

History repeated itself. What Tex had done once before, now he did again.

Sturmer was up against one of the fastest men on the draw in Texas. As Tex crashed into the saddle behind the ex-Nazi, his hand streaked for that gun — knocked Sturmer's descending hand out of the way and drew it.

Once before Sturmer had been a prisoner for two days while his own revolver was pressed to his ribs by one or another of Tex's party. This time, however, Tex employed other tactics — this time they mightn't understand, these *partizans*; that if he were shot, their leader might be shot too. Anyway understanding might come too late for both him and Sturmer.

Tex shoved the revolver into his belt. Then he exerted all his strength wrestling with that ferociously fighting Legion captain, while the horse reared around in alarm. But Sturmer was at a disadvantage; his back was towards his adversary.

Desperation gave Tex superhuman strength. With a mighty heave he plucked the struggling Sturmer clean out of his saddle and flung him head down across his back. Somehow he got Sturmer's head crooked painfully under his right arm, while his left hand gripped behind the knee of Sturmer's right leg.

It was an undignified position for the Legion captain and Sturmer shouted in fury and fought with reckless strength to release himself from that hold. Tex kicked heels into his horse's sides, steering with his knees and bringing it running on to the hard, rocky trail.

Tex saw startled, bearded faces look up from behind the rocks as he raced level with them. The *partizans* certainly hadn't expected this. Then their guns came round to cover him — but too late.

When their sights came up on to that target, they found themselves aiming at their leader, held upside down as a shield behind the Texan. They held their fire. Instead a few ran to their horses, determined to follow where their captain went.

Tex heard hoof beats. Then his attention was taken up by the lead that began to come in his direction. Sturmer was trying to kick him, trying to punch his ribs in. Tex just gripped harder on that small head and made it so painful that Sturmer was obliged to stop being awkward.

Then the bullets stopped coming down the defile towards him, Tex realized vaguely, for all that there was plenty of rifle-fire higher up the defile. Almost immediately he understood. Elly, Rube, Dimmy and 'brahim were firing upon the startled Legion renegades! That must have been a terrible shock to Ca-ca and his men, to find that while engaged with one enemy, their other had crawled behind them.

That took their fire away from Tex, and he was able to ride up the steep slope towards that shelf on which Louie lay without any further danger.

But it also brought all the *partizans* out from hiding, and now they came pouring up after him, urging their mounts into their fastest speed in an effort to draw level with Texas.

That could only have been in a matter of seconds, for on that steep, rocky trail a doubly laden horse was severely handicapped. Tex frantically urged it on, all the while grimly holding on to his enemy. At this moment, ironically, Sturmer was saving his life, for with the Legion officer on his back, between him and the renegade Arabs, they couldn't shoot the ex-cowboy.

But Tex, feeling the labouring strength of the horse beneath him, knew that he couldn't win this race. Almost up to the shelf, he could hear the savage, exultant yells of his pursuers. Five seconds more and they would be alongside with those dreaded, sweeping swords of theirs . . .

Louie stood up on the edge of the trail. Tex shouted, 'Grab a stirrup an' hang on, Louie!' Though he knew it was hopeless. He couldn't save himself now, much less his former comrade.

But Louie shook his head. Louie wasn't going on this trip. Louie was going to wipe out some old debts, instead.

Tex saw him lift his Lebel and sight it past him. It plumed white smoke. A swift movement and a new round was in the breech. Again Louie fired.

That turned the *partizans*. Probably it was the shock of seeing a Legionnaire where they hadn't expected one that deterred them. Probably they thought this was a trap, that there might be more than one man on this shelf where those eight horses were.

Harsh voices shouted in alarm, and they turned their beasts and ran back under cover.

Louie was dead, though, before they reached it. One of the *partizans* must have ripped off a shot that ended Louie's inglorious life.

'But he died to give me a chance.' was all Tex could think. 'He wiped off the wrongs he did agen us with that action.'

Now Tex could go at an easier pace up the defile. There wasn't much firing now. Jacques Quelclos, the dwarf was lying across the trail, dead. Ca-ca's boots protruded from behind a rock, and he didn't move, either. Cheauvin the Belgian was rocking in agony, his hands to his head.

Petrie, who had aspired one day to become a chief executioner, was standing with his hands held stiffly aloft murder on his face for all that. The Bulgar was to one side and with him La Femme, both in attitudes of surrender. Legionnaire Joe Ellighan was crouching in the middle of the trail, his Lebel covering them.

Elly shouted, 'Keep goin' Tex!' as Tex's overburdened mount panted past him. Tex nodded and kept going. Round the bend were the rest of the party, the girls already in the saddle, the men retiring and grabbing horses and mounting in a great confusion of movement.

Nicky shouted, 'Nice work, Tex!'

Tex pulled the Legion officer over his shoulder, slammed him face down across his horse before him, and stuck the officer's own revolver into Sturmer's ribs.

Then he rode in among his friends. They were delighted to see him, and the men leaned out of their saddles to slap him on the back. Mahfra called a greeting in Arabic, and he caught the flash of her smile. She was looking at Nicky and Tex and understanding.

In that milling confusion Rube suddenly shouted, 'Hold hard. Elly hasn't got a horse!'

He rode across to where Mahfra was mounted on a beast. He was going to lift her on to his own, when suddenly 'brahim, the sheik's son who wished to become an American, was there. Mahfra looked at him, then smiled and held out her arms. 'brahim took her and set her before him.

Tex heard him say, carelessly — too carelessly, 'I will look after her, Rube.'

The former horse-wrangler and cowboy was satisfied. He seemed to have got out of a complication there. They began to ride away, just as a grinning Elly ran up and leapt on to the spare horse.

He called, 'There ain't no hurry, pards.'

It was confident, reassuring, and they pulled down to a slow trot on the steep ascent. Behind them a rifle cracked out, but the bullet wasn't coming their way. Then a steady stream of fire could be heard more distantly, and there was the scream of bullets ricochetting within the confines of that rocky chasm.

Joe Ellighan, the boy from Brooklyn, grinned as big a grin as he'd ever created. He jerked his thumb back towards where the battle was raging. 'Them guys,' he yapped happily. 'The Bulgar, La Femme an' Chopper Petrie. Them guys is havin' to hold back them *partizans* for us. Now, ain't that a laugh?'

But the renegades wouldn't be laughing, Tex knew. They had no horses upon which to flee; escape on foot was out of the question. So all they could do was fight back against men who would take their heads the moment they got up to them.

It was in their favour — Tex's and his

party. Every minute that the *partizans* were held up gave them a lead on their terrible pursuers. Two or three more hours and they would be over the mountains and on to the Libyan desert beyond, 'brahim assured them. And in two-three hours night would be upon them, and then they could lose any pursuers out on that dreary, scrub-covered waste.

It was a pleasant prospect, a far better one than any of them could have anticipated, half an hour ago — even five minutes ago, Tex thought. Here they were, miraculously safe, having turned the tables on two vicious sets of enemies, and with the prize he was after, ex-Nazi Sturmer, a prisoner in their midst

Tex said, frankly, 'I don't know how it happened.' Nicky was riding by his side, holding his hand 'brahim was whispering to Mahfra, and the Arab girl was dropping her eyes modestly, but smiling and liking it.

Rube turned and looked back at Tex. He said, 'It was good planning,' and plainly he took credit for most of it himself. Tex let it go at that. Rube was a good boy; he could have the credit.

Some time later, though, he told them about Louie. He said, 'He died helpin' us. We won't think bad of the guy after that.'

He told them how Louie had refused help, had told him to ride on, and had turned back the *partizans* for a few vital seconds with some well-directed rifle-fire.

Nicky whispered, 'He was so ill, too. I never liked him, but . . . ' She shrugged.

'He kinda showed there was sand in him, after all.'

Elegant was deliberating. Finally he gave his opinion. 'That was a guy who rose above his birthplace. That guy was good enough to come from Brooklyn.'

And the way Elegant paused when he said it, plainly he felt it the most fitting epitaph he could utter.

Long shadows from the bare, craggy mountain wall to their right gave them welcome shadow. In an hour they were on the summit, with the sound of battle a mere splutter of faint crackling sounds coming occasionally to their ears.

Mervin Petrie and his desperate companions were still holding the pass against their enemies, apparently.

They reined in, where the chasm through the mountain began to descend. They looked ahead, across four hundred miles of dreary desert.

Four hundred miles and then they would reach the sea. Even then they would not be safe, but now they didn't count the odds against their being permitted to board a vessel out of the Mediterranean. If they survived the dangers, natural and man-made, of that long desert journey, they felt they would accomplish the next leg in their travels.

Nicky looked at the big Texan and said, softly, 'It's going to be fun, Tex, riding across Libya.'

He smiled and said, softly, back, 'So long as we keep together, honey . . . '

Sturmer, lying uncomfortably across that horse, heard them, though. He was quite still, reserving his strength, thinking.

Thinking that in four hundred miles a man might escape.

THE END

TOMORROW, UTOPIA

Steve Hayes and David Whitehead

In Washington a high-ranking politician is murdered, whilst in Central Africa, a new virus is killing thousands of male victims. And on the internet, a group known as The Utopians grows in power. Is there a connection between all these things? Homicide Detective Ben Hicks, however, has his own problems. Meanwhile, Pentagon cryptologist Hunter McCormack witnesses the murder of a politician. Now the killers are out to silence *her* . . . and no one believes she saw the killing. Except Ben . . .

THE PLOT AGAINST SHERLOCK HOLMES

Gary Lovisi

When Sherlock Holmes finds himself enmeshed in the most deadly case of his career, it threatens to bring terrible doom upon him and his friend Doctor John H. Watson. A deadly nemesis from his past, a most vile and evil villain, has returned to England to wreak his revenge for past deeds. He unleashes a dastardly plot, which begins with a shocking murder in Whitechapel and causes Inspector Lestrade to believe that Jack the Ripper has returned . . .

CLOSELY KNIT IN SCARLATT

Ardath Mayhar

Olive, 'The Knit Lady,' is an unlikely secret agent. A professional assassin and in her sixties, she had been quietly recruited by 'The Brokers.' Now she is hired to kidnap and kill retired British agent Benjamin Scarlatt, but Olive has scruples. And when an Islamic terrorist group takes over the cruise ship on which both she and Scarlatt are travelling, she fights back with knitting needle, scalpel and plastic explosives — proving that it's dangerous to underestimate Little Old Ladies!